Yesterday is Gone

By HJ Bellus

Yesterday is Gone

Limitless Publishing, LLC
Kailua, HI 96734
www.limitlesspublishing.com

Formatting: Limitless Publishing

ISBN-13: 978-1-64034-423-5
ISBN-10: 1-64034-423-3

Dedication

To all of those who are brave enough to give second
chances one final shot.

Prologue

Jules

"I give you the class of…"

Everything blurs in and out. The other sixty students stand and toss their caps in their air. Mine remains on my head. There's nothing to celebrate. My future was crushed with a few ignorant words. *This can't happen. It will ruin everything. Fuck, Jules, take care of it.*

It was in that moment everything crystalized, picture perfect. I'd take care of it. Jessie would be free to conquer the world like he'd been destined to do. His cold and calculated words strike my heart with each beat. Never would I think my best friend and the love of my life would handle the news this way. We've been by each other's sides since kindergarten.

Jessie is laser-focused on his full-ride football scholarship to Michigan. It's no excuse. He crushed me without a second thought. Each word of my valedictorian speech was muted with heartache and sorrow. It was the moment I'd been looking forward to since my freshman year.

The only thing that got me through it was my Nanny Jane. She is the one person who has always loved me without a second thought. Papa Jack beamed as wide as she did watching me deliver my speech. I kept focused on their two loving faces.

She took me in when my mom gave me up. It seems I'm repeating the cycle getting knocked up in high school. Tears prick at the corners of my eyes. My current situation isn't too far off from my beginning.

Nanny's son, Dalton, enlisted in the Army and shipped off right after graduation. His high school sweetheart, Hailey, wanted nothing to do with the child growing in her womb. Nanny supported her the full nine months and then adopted me. She gained a new granddaughter and lost her only son to war all in the same year.

"Hey, ready to go to the lock-in party?" Tessi nudges my shoulder, bouncing up and down on her stilettos.

I shake my head. "I'm not feeling good. Nanny and Papa have a small party set up for me at home."

It's a lie. There's no party. I'd planned on going to the lock-in, spending the entire night in Jessie's arms.

"Are you okay?" Tessi's face turns concerned for a few seconds.

I nod, swallowing down all the shame and pain. "I'm fine. Want to get in all the time with them before Jessie and I head to Michigan."

"That's next week, right?"

"Yeah."

"Well, sister, you better schedule me in for some time, too." She kisses my cheek and takes off without a care or worry in the world.

That should be me.

Clutching my diploma in my hand, I weave through the crowd with my head ducked down. A few family friends pat me on the back and stop me for a hug.

"There she is." Carolyn scoops me up in a hug. "Wanted to snap a picture of you and Jessie before you head out."

I look up to Jessie standing in front of me, his strong jawline taut and his eyes full of remorse. Words can never be taken back. He may be regretting them, but it's too late.

"Now, get together." Carolyn nudges us. "We need Tessi and Brady. Where did those two run off to?"

"You're not going to find them in this crowded gym, honey. Just take the picture. The gang will be home every school break, and you can get their picture then," Jessie's dad grumbles clearly over the noise and the stifling heat in the gymnasium.

The gang. Everything is ending tonight. Tessi, my best friend, Brady, Jessie's best, and the two of us are tight. Even though Tessi and Brady can't stand each other most of the time, anyone could find the four of us causing trouble all over town and having a damn good time.

Jessie slings an arm over my shoulders. His rich musky and woodsy scent showers down on me. I find myself cuddling into his side for one last memory. I battle the tears back. It's a losing war. I glance up to Jessie's whiskey-colored eyes. The ones that have loved me and kept me safe over the years. It's almost as if he's a stranger to me now.

His thick dark hair is tousled, his graduation cap missing, tossed in the sea of the rest of them, and his dimples are on full display. It's not a happy moment for me. It's a goodbye. Jessie leans down and glides his lips over my forehead before placing a gentle kiss.

Then his lips are at the shell of my ear. He kisses me lightly there, too.

"Jules, I'm sorry. So fucking sorry. This isn't the right time. God, this is killing me."

This isn't my Jessie talking to me right now. Greed and a taste of the limelight have destroyed him. He's not thinking straight. I could beg and plead him. The thing is you can never take back words, and he struck me with the worst of them. He made it clear where I stand as he starts his new journey in life.

I reach up on my tiptoes and leave one long, lingering kiss on his lips before walking away. He grabs my hand pulling me back to him; his strong arms wrap around me, tugging me to his chest.

"Take care of it and come to Michigan. I need you, Jules."

Lifelong love turns to hate in a matter of seconds. I plant my palms on his chest and shove off him.

"Best of luck in life, Jessie."

I don't let one single tear fall until I'm in the dark of the parking lot. And I don't stop until they dry up.

Chapter 1

Jules

Every flag on Main Street is half-staff in honor of the late Senator Jack Jones, the reason I'm back in my hometown. It's been over five years since I left the night of graduation and never looked back.

My chest tightens as each flag goes by. The tears of sorrow I've held back fall freely. Papa Jack will forever be missed. He loved visiting California every month even though he pissed and moaned about all the damn traffic and people. It was when he was on the beach with Nana's at their beach house and at peace with a smile consuming his face that I knew it was all smoke.

"What in the hell is going on there?" I whisper to myself.

The parking lot to Gravy Dave's is overflowing with vehicles. Shit, cars even line Main Street. Somebody is having one hell of a celebration. I let out a rush of breath, thankful it's dark. I'm not ready for this. The sad fact is I'll never be prepared for it.

Everything looks the same and different at the same time. I slow down, taking it all in. The movie theater is boarded up. The marquee light flickers dimly, advertising the upcoming county fair and rodeo in one month. Even in the faint glow of the street lights, I can see the beauty of the blossoming petunia baskets that adorn each pole on the main drag.

Old memories of cruising Main in my old '79 Chevy attack me. Even though I don't want to smile, I find myself doing so. This town was my everything at one point in time. It seems it can pull me right back in, making me feel like a teenager at heart. The only beauty shop in town, Solutions, comes into view. The same tacky sign from the '80s remains bold in a fresh coat of paint.

I learned several lessons in that old building, from you never look like the picture in the magazine to how to roll a condom on a dick. I snort, thinking to myself how I miserably failed that lesson.

The other part of Main Street that makes me sick, besides the half-staff flags, is that the old "O-So-Good" drive-in had been refurbished into a credit union. It was the hopping place we all swarmed to after every football victory. The owner insisted on curbside service complete with the trays that rested on our windows. Every time we'd end up on Jessie's tailgate, swarmed by friends and sipping on ice cold sodas.

The soft glow of street lights fades off into the distance as I hit the country roads, buzzing by the familiar lights of farms and homes. The years have drifted by, yet I can put a name to every home. Before too long, Jessie's old home flies by, and then I'm pulling down the mile-long drive to my childhood home. Papa's old red truck is parked in his spot right outside the garage. He's always had so much junk in there that I never remember a time anyone could park in it. Nana's white Cadillac dutifully sits next to Papa's truck.

The pang of guilt and sorrow strikes. Their monthly visit wouldn't make this trip back home any better. I may have run, but never from them. We kept our connection over the years. I stop my mid-size Toyota RAV4 hybrid right next to the entry gate along the chain link fence and smile, remembering Papa's grumbles over my foreign rig. The porch light welcomes me home. But it's the three worn and loved rocking chairs on the porch that give me the strength to take the next step.

Chapter 2

Jules

"Let her sleep." I tap Whit's nose. "Go on out and run through the sprinklers until lunch is ready."

"But Nana said we could have a spa day." My little spitfire stomps her foot.

Jesus, can you take the wheel now?

I glance over to Papa's Farm Bureau coffee mug. The same one he'd sip his coffee out of since I was Whit's age. Praying to all gods they would give me the strength, I kneel down to Whit's level.

"Baby girl, Nan is super sad and needs her rest. You can have a girls' spa when she wakes up."

Whit tilts her head in thought while ruffling the layers of her lime green tutu. Her hot pink polka-dot bikini top entirely clashes with it. "But painting toes makes everyone happy."

"Want me to start counting and then go batshit-crazy-level mom?"

She pinches her lips together. "I'll be out playing in the sprinklers, Momma."

Whit rushes out in a blur of lime green. I slap my palms on the counter, hating the fact I resorted to my best friend Lydia's tactics. Damn her! Guarantee if she were here, she'd be gloating about the fact she's the number one aunt.

I rifle through the fridge, dumping casserole dishes from friends and neighbors. Some things never change, and that's horrendous casseroles made by shitty cooks. I have no clue how many times growing up we tried to stomach food from Mrs. Wade. Nan finally learned to accept the gift with a smile and then scrape it out into the trashcan.

All the while, I keep an eye on the roast browning in a cast iron skillet. Nan couldn't be happy about the fact I'm about to toss it in an Instant Pot for dinner. It's grilled cheese, pickles, and store-bought potato salad for lunch. I'm armed and ready for Nana's protest over Reese potato salad. I'm dealing with her and everything I can the best I know how, and that means store-bought ready-to-eat food.

Before long, I'm cleaning out cabinets, tossing outdated seasonings. I lose track of time and the fact Whit's sandwiches have been done for some time. It's a trick I've learned over the years of being a mother. If the princess is playing and happy, let her enjoy it. I continue sorting the kitchen, knowing damn well there will be hell to pay.

"C'use me, sir. We ain't buying." Whit's sweet voice drifts in through the kitchen window.

I brush my hands off on the delicately embroidered tea towel and peer out the window. My heart ceases to beat. The man who crushed me waltzes up the cracked sidewalk. No. No. No. I thought I'd have more time.

Jessie's deep, familiar chuckle echoes in the country breeze. He rakes his hand through his hair. He's aged to perfection. Now a sculpted, tight beard frames his face; the same scar runs through his right eyebrow; his olive skin tone still mesmerizes me.

Jessie tucks his hands in his pockets and dips his chin for a brief moment before responding. "Here to see Jane. Told her I'd come by to change water and mow."

Whit dances right up to Jessie. She covers her eyes, shading them from the sun, one hand on her hip.

"What's your name, mister?"

"Jessie." He nods.

She promptly sticks out her hand. "Hi, I'm Whit Jane Jones."

Jessie freezes. Long moments float by before he clears his throat and extends his hand. His eyes flare wide as their hands connect.

"Nice to meet you," she chirps.

Jessie doesn't respond or drop her hand.

"You're 'pose to say, 'Nice to meet you, too, Whit Jane Jones.' It's the polite thing to do." She dances in place, growing impatient.

Jessie's voice cracks with emotion as he slowly speaks each word. "Nice to meet you, too, Whit Jane Jones."

"Momma's making lunch. Let's go get it." She wiggles her hand free and darts toward the porch, yelling like a banshee. "Mom, a Jessie is here to water your grass."

With hesitant steps, I walk to the front door. I clench my fists at my sides, swallow hard, and push it open. Jessie hasn't moved, and I don't take a step towards him.

"Pee, pee, pee." Whit rushes underneath my outstretched arm, holding the screen door open.

Once she disappears into the house, Jessie clears his throat and walks up to the bottom step.

"Jules." He nods.

The man I loved for so many years and have hated for the last five years stares at me like a day hasn't passed.

"Nana's sleeping. You can come back when she's awake or go about whatever you need to do."

"I'm sorry, Jules." He pauses for long beats before continuing on. "About your grandpa. He was a good guy."

My shoulders relax a tick. If he was about to apologize for turning his back on me, it would have destroyed the last shred of control I have at this moment. I nod, acknowledging him.

"Going to eat, Momma," Whit sings, skipping behind me.

I turn for a brief second. "Did you wash your hands?"

"Like a hundred times." Whit rolls her eyes.

The sound of Jessie's laughter forces my attention back on him. My glare erases the smile on his face. He tucks his chin to his chest, toeing some pebbles on the cracked sidewalk with his cowboy boots.

"She has my eyes."

He speaks so gently and quietly, I'm not sure I

was supposed to hear him. Hearing Jessie acknowledge his daughter for the first time guts me and leaves me speechless. I do the only thing I can, and that's step back into the house and slam the screen door. The main one follows. There will never be enough barriers between that man and me. It's painful enough as it is, knowing I'm tied to him forever.

The nights I had to make up stories about Whit's dad when she asked where he was kept the iron-clad barrier protecting my heart.

"Who was that?" Nana rounds the corner in a housecoat.

"Jessie!" Whit hollers from the dining room table.

"I'm sorry," Nana whispers.

I shrug and go to her, hugging her tight. "Don't be. I'm here for you. Probably should've come home a long time ago."

"I might be selfish, Jules, but it feels so good to have you here. I just wish it wasn't..." Her voice cracks, and she can't continue.

I rock her back and forth until her tears dry up.

Chapter 3

Jules

I make sure I'm up first thing in the morning even though I only got in a few hours of sleep. Even seeing Jessie wasn't enough torture—my childhood room sealed the deal. It's the same as it was when I was growing up.

Garth Brooks posters plaster the walls, mixed in with a few New Kids on the Block. Trophies, pom-poms, and old pictures cover the rest of the space. Not to mention the Pepto-Bismol comforter I just had to have with all the lace and frills. Whit thought it was excellent.

Her enthusiasm gave me the courage to walk into the space. She curled up next to me in the bed and was out in moments. Her rhythmic breathing and light snoring were the only things that calmed me. I stroked her hair, reliving every memory I once cherished.

The moment I dozed off, it felt like my eyes had been closed for five minutes before the rooster began crowing. I crawled out of bed, tucking Whit down in the blankets.

Morning coffee was always Papa's thing. That man lived on coffee. Drank it all day, every day. Nana always had a fresh pot brewing for him every morning. He'd read the paper, sipping on the hot joe while Nana would put together her to-do list for the day. Didn't matter how old I was, it was always the same scene.

The bitter aroma of coffee fills the kitchen when I enter it. Nana is in her housecoat, curlers in her hair, while she frantically jots down her to-do list.

"Morning." I wrap my arms around from behind and kiss her cheek.

"You're up early, Firecracker."

I smile at the nickname.

"Smelled the coffee." I snag a mug from the cupboard over her shoulder and fill a cup.

Nana remains in the spot for long moments before grabbing her lavender-colored Avon mug and Papa's. She fills both up, adding one sugar cube and a splash of milk to hers, leaving Papa's mug straight black. Tears fill her eyes as she sets both on the table.

I reach over and grab her hand. She doesn't say a word as she continues writing her list. The most influential woman I've ever known sits before me, shattered. My heart clenches at the scene. She experienced the strongest love known, and now it's about to destroy her. I crave to fix it all, but I can't. There were so many late nights and early mornings where she held me when I was in pain. She was always there. Now it's my turn. No matter how painful it is to be back in this town, I'll be here for her.

I grab a piece of paper from the table and flip it over, picking up my own pen. Writing has become an escape for me. An avenue I never thought of until I was left in the world all alone. It's become so much more. My passion and outlet out of my reality. I create all sorts of stories, letting the ink bleed on the paper.

"How am I going to wake up every morning without him?" Nana's pen topples to the table. Her wrinkled hand tremors.

When I glance up at her, silent tears roll down her face. I'm up and at her side holding her, absorbing each one of her shudders.

"I don't know, Nana. I don't know. What I do know is that Whit and I are here for you. We aren't going anywhere. Lean on us. We got you." I run my hand up and down her back.

When she's able to talk, it crushes me. "You hate it here. I know you can't live here and have a life somewhere else. I can't do this, Jules."

"Hey." I drop to my knees. "Listen to me. You're right, this might be the last place on earth I want to be. The thing is I'm not leaving you. I don't care about the rest of the shit. You are the only thing that matters."

"I wasn't truthful yesterday," she admits.

I crane my neck, urging her to go on.

"Jessie and your papa did a lot together. The older we got, the more he came around to help out. He never saw pictures of Whit. It was nice to have him around and helping us out."

I'd be a liar if I said that didn't sting like a bitch. If I could see past all the anger and hatred, I'd be thankful Jessie was here for them.

"Okay." I gulp down a lump of emotion clogging my throat. "I'm okay with that. He helped you guys when you needed it. I can't be pissed over that. It's going to take time to adjust to life here. The bottom line remains the same—I'm here for you as long as you need me."

The tears continue. The heartache races forward, and all I can do is hold on.

"Momma." A sleepy voice creeps in from the hall, followed by a messy brown-haired girl wiping the sleep from her eyes. "Is it bacon time?"

It takes Whit a few moments to gain her bearings. Nana rushes to wipe away her tears. Whit's too smart not to catch on.

"Oh, Nana," she coos, racing over to her and climbing up into her lap.

Whit's tiny hands clutch her cheeks. Smooth, youthful skin pressed against worn, wise, wrinkled skin. Whit's chipped hot pink fingernails smooth circles on Nana's cheek.

"You gonna be okay?" Whit nods her head.

"I am now." Nana wraps her up in a tight hug.

Whit throws her arms around her neck. I lean down and kiss the top of Nana's head. Everything is going to be okay. Papa was our foundation and strength. He made us into the women we are today. We might not know the way he fed the cows, planted the hay, or harvested, but we sure in the hell will take care of it.

"I'll fix you girls up some oatmeal." I squeeze

Nana's shoulder before walking away.

"Bacon time." Whit's head pops up.

"Whit, oatmeal."

"Momma, I hate that stuff."

We go back and forth for extended minutes. Whit has bartered a tutu and her favorite doll by this point for some crispy bacon.

"That's it." Nana slaps the table. "I've cooked a hot breakfast the last forty years of my life. I want bacon too, dammit, but I don't want to cook it. Get dressed, ladies."

I groan, smacking my face. Bed, blankets, and sleep are all I want. Zapping two bowls of oatmeal and sneaking back up to Nana's bed for a few hours of sleep sounds more delicious than any breakfast food.

"Yes! Now you're talking." Whit leaps from Nana's lap and races upstairs.

I send a playful glare to Nana. She shrugs.

"Let's get out of here," she says.

***

"Let me wipe some off, honey." I reach towards Whit with a spare hoodie in our car.

"No, Mom." She bats away my hand and slides out of her booster.

"She's fine." Nana waves me off.

The two trot into Gravy Dave's hand in hand. Goddamn Avon. It was the first thing Whit got into today, and let me tell you, Nana has a room devoted to her love of Avon. They smell like two-bit whores even though Whit swore up and down she only put on two squirts of perfume. Who knows how old the damn bottle was? I put the brakes on at fire engine red lipstick. The blush and light eyeshadow were enough. I lost the battle when the both of them came out with lipstick on.

The sight of the two would be comical any other day, but I'm exhausted mentally and physically. The saving grace was Nana applied the lipstick, so it wasn't smeared everywhere.

I soak in the moment of silence and peace in the car, dropping my forehead to the steering wheel. My heart throbs in pain along with my head. The tears don't come. I don't have time for them. It's my turn to be the strong one. It would be so easy to let my eyes flutter close and drift off into sleep, even with the harsh steering wheel pressing into my skin.

***

Jessie

"Summer camp starts in a week. We are keeping the same schedule as last year?" Brady asks, thumping the tabletop with his fingers.

"Yeah." I jerk my chin.

"We have more freshmen this year. Eli said there's a handful that will easily be able to play varsity," he continues.

I nod, staring out the window, fucking haunted from last night. Always knew it was inevitable for Jules to roll back into town. Been hoping for quite some time that it would've been by now. Getting injured and being sent home from the big leagues was a bitch slap, a cold, harsh one I needed. Not a day has gone by that I haven't regretted my words to Jules. There ain't one excuse I can come up with. I was a cocky, arrogant asshole who let the promise of money and fame get to me.

The moment I signed with Michigan, I changed. Hell, I'd always been the hometown's favorite on and off the field, but with that extra notch in my belt, it ruined me. It didn't matter that when I won the first state title, Jules was by my side, and it was her I wanted to hug first. We were best friends since we could walk. I fell in love with her in sixth grade. She was my everything. That is until the ugly monster of greed struck me dumb.

Her voice speaking the words that had the power to threaten everything still haunts my dreams. I reacted. I didn't think it through or even act rationally. I destroyed us. I obliterated a piece of myself that night. I've never been the same.

A diminished bit of ash sparked back to life when that little girl came bouncing up to me. Her wild brown curls and sassy personality struck a chord. Knew it the moment I saw her she was mine. She's Jules' mini-me, but her eyes are mine.

Stayed up all damn night last night wondering how in the hell I'm just finding out I have a daughter. Yeah, Jules hasn't been back to town since high school graduation, but her grandparents have been here the whole time. Hell, been working real close with Jack the last year. Jane invited me over for weekly Sunday dinners along with my parents. They've attended every home football game, rooting on the local high school.

It fucking baffles me, leaving only one option, and that's Jules never wanted to talk to me again. I told her to take care of it, and she did. I grimace at the memory. It's not what I had in mind. And that makes me a fucking monster after meeting Whit. My girl.

"Jessie, what the hell is going on?" Brady slaps the table.

I look over to him, realizing I'm rubbing out an ache in my chest. I shake my head. "Nothing."

"Bullshit." Brady leans forward. "We're heading into a season coming off our third state title, and your head is long fucking gone. Was it the proposal last night?"

That question sends a bucket of ice-cold water over my spine. My life is so fucked up right now I don't know where to begin analyzing it to dig myself out of this endless hole.

The bell above the restaurant's door shrills, gaining everyone's attention. The one person who can shed light in my life right now prances in, hand in hand with her grandma. The little spitfire shines in her zebra leggings, neon orange tutu, sparkly shirt, and ballet flats. She twirls around in a circle, holding the tip of Jane's finger. When she stops, I see the make-up covering her face.

It makes me smile. She obviously got into Jane's Avon stash. Everyone nods and greets Jane. She introduces Whit with pride. You can see the questions on everyone's faces. It's enough the town just lost one of their heroes. I'm thankful no one dares ask about Whit. It's a shock, and I'll beat down any asshole who opens their mouth.

I look back to the window, peering out to the street. That's when I see Jules slumped over, her head pressed into the steering wheel in her fancy car. I've done this to her. She left town because of me. Missed out on years with her grandpa all because of me. The guilt is too much. It's enough to make me want to quit living.

"Jessie!"

I swivel my attention over to Whit, who's bounding toward me. She scrambles up into the booth and perches on her knees.

"What are you doing here?" She wrinkles her button nose, pointing at me.

A chuckle escapes me. "Well, I'm eating breakfast. What are you doing here?"

She plops a hand on her hip.

"It's bacon time, duh!" She settles in the booth next to me, her feet dangling and kicking with her elbows perched on the tabletop. "Momma wanted to force me to eat oatmeal. Gag. Nana busted us out of there."

Brady bottlenecks his gaze between the both of us, easily putting the large-size puzzle pieces together. He was my best friend in high school, well, besides Jules. It was always the three of us, plus Brady's nemesis, Tessi, riding together in my truck, attending parties, and causing chaos. He's asked over the years about Jules. Hell, did everything to pry something from me. I never gave him a morsel.

"Oatmeal ain't bad." I shrug.

"Jessie." Whit pats my shoulder, getting my

attention even though I'm already staring down at her. "Is there a dance studio here? I've got to dance. I danced four times a week in California. I'll die if I don't."

"Yeah, there's one."

She hops back up on her knees. Damn, the kid doesn't sit still. She helps herself to a piece of bacon on my plate. I don't miss the fact she drags it through the maple syrup. It's the only way to eat it in my opinion. It always grossed Jules out. Whit chomps down on the end of it while a drizzle of syrup drips down her front.

"Will you take me? Momma is stressed out. It's constipated." She shrugs. "Nana is sad, and you're the only other person I know."

I bite down on my bottom lip at her substitution for "complicated." It makes me wonder how much she knows about the situation. The words she uses and the way she rattles on lets me know this girl, my girl, is damn smart.

The bell rattles once more. Whit whips her head in the direction of the door. Her curls fly everywhere. I spot a hair tie hanging loosely on the end and the syrup-covered bacon tangling in the mess.

"Momma." Whit flags down Jules with what's left of my bacon. "Over here."

Jules smiles at the sound of her daughter's voice. It falls as quickly as it appeared when we make eye contact. She tightens her jaw and stiffens her shoulders. It takes her long moments before she walks over to us.

"Where's Nana?" she asks in a controlled voice.

"Over there talking to friends." The bacon is wielded once again. "Momma, Jessie said he's taking me to dance classes."

Oh, fuck! I clear my throat. I don't have the chance to comment before Jules ushers Whit out of the booth.

"C'mon, let's go join Nana. Tell Jessie bye." Jules adjusts Whit's tutu.

"Bye, Jessie." A toothy grin flashes at me.

"See ya, Whit." I can't help the smile that covers my face. That girl makes everything better.

Jules spins on her heels. I'm up and on my feet before I can think. I grab her upper arm, urging her to turn around. She doesn't. I lean in, pressing my chest to her back. We have the attention of the entire restaurant, which in small town language means this will spread to the next county by lunch. The scent of grapefruit and lilies hits me. Her smell. Her favorite perfume, Happy. She still wears it. Discovered it our junior year in high school and damned near bathed in the stuff.

"It's not like that," I whisper in her ear, not letting go of her arm. "She bounced into our booth and asked if there was a dance studio. I said yes, she stole a piece of my bacon, and that's it."

Jules nods, remaining frozen.

"She dipped it in syrup. We need to talk, Jules." I let go and step back.

She whirls around. I take a second to soak her in. It's not the right place or time, but I can't help myself. Tight-ass black jeans hug her lean, tall legs, brown leather boots roam up to right below her kneecap, and a white tank top is all she has on top.

Her nipples hard and poking through let me know I still do something to her whether she likes it or not.

"Stay away from us," she seethes. "We have nothing to talk about."

"Jules," Brady belts from the booth. "How the hell have you been?"

Jules peers over at him and offers him a gentle smile, more than I got from her. Fuck no, I don't deserve one, but doesn't mean it doesn't hurt all the same.

"Good. Been better. Have a nice day." She ends her sentence with a tight smile before walking away.

Brady slides out of the booth, pats my shoulder, and shakes his head. "That's what has your head so fucked up. Makes sense. Congrats, Daddio."

I tug my wallet out of the back of my jeans and toss two twenties on the table. "Keep your mouth shut about this. Jules doesn't need any more stress. The death of her grandpa is enough."

"Anyone that sees that little girl will know. It's a small town. Better be prepared for hell, man."

"Shut the fuck up," I growl. "We need to get to thrashing hay."

Chapter 4

Jules

"Go!" Nana pushes me out the front door. "We will be just fine."

I dig my heels in. It's been one hell of a long day. Yesterday morning was enough to piss me off for an entire year. Today was enough to drain the remaining energy from my body. Picking out caskets and headstones was hell at its finest. It was picking out Papa's best suit for him to be buried in that did me in.

It was the moment I cracked wide open in the bottom of his closet surrounded by his lingering scent. Nana was wiped from the day's events. I had stepped up and handled the rest of them. I cried myself to sleep wrapped in Papa's flannel shirt until Whit woke me when she was up from her nap.

Tomorrow will be worse. I can't even begin to process how when I'm at an all-time low today. I want to be there when he's dressed. Papa was damn particular about his tie and how his suit fit. It's something he picked up from being in the U.S. Senate. His favorite town boots still need to be shined, and all I want to do is give up.

"Go!" Nana hollers one more time.

Tessi waves from the gate, jumping up and down and squealing. We ran into her today when leaving the funeral home on Main Street. She was ecstatic, over the moon to see me again. She had her two children with her and didn't stop rattling on. I felt guilty as hell because all I wanted to do was hide.

Each step down the cracked sidewalk is massive. Everything weighs down on me. Whit went to bed early from all the excitement of the past few days. Any other night this happens, I'm either crawling in bed with her or writing. She hasn't stopped asking when Jessie is picking her up for dance. Each time his name comes from her lips, I die on the inside. It's inevitable. I'm going to have to share, and that's something I've never prepared myself for.

"You look amazing, Jules!" Tessi squeals and wraps me up in a hug.

I step back, looking up and down at my outfit—short cut-offs, a black tank top, and strappy sandals. Nana tried over and over to get me to put some make-up on. I refused, tying my hair up in a messy bun.

"You do, too," I reply.

It's not a lie. Tessi still contains her youthful glow. Long blonde hair, banging body, and her smile. You'd never be able to tell she's had two kids, Lenny and Jillian, who are three and one and a half, or at least that's what I remember from earlier today. Hell, maybe it's four and two, and their names are Lance and Jennifer.

"Let's go." She rounds the front of her monstrous, blacked-out Escalade.

I crawl in, exhausted and three seconds from busting out of the car. The leather seat swallows me whole. I throw my head back and close my eyes. I hear Tessi's door slam and feel her hand on my thigh.

"You're not doing good."

I shake my head, keeping my eyes closed.

"Honey, let's go get drunk."

I roll my head toward her and pry one eye open. "I can't even tell you the last time I was drunk. Pretty sure it was high school."

"Do you not drink anymore?"

"I do. A glass of wine or two a couple times a week, but being a single mom doesn't allow time for it."

Tessi's face falls. I know she's hurt. Saw it when she met Whit today. We were tight back in the day, and then I disappeared.

"I'm sorry, Tessi, it's complicated." I lift my head.

"She's Jessie's. I get that. Didn't take all but two seconds to realize that one." She reaches up and squeezes my hand. "Can't imagine what you're going through with losing the man who was basically your dad and then having to come back here."

"I had to leave." I think about revealing how Jessie reacted that night. It's not something I've ever bragged about, and I'm sure as hell not proud. It also feels private and like something that should stay between us. It's what forced me out of this town, and I'm tired of it eating me alive. "Jessie basically told me to take care of it and meet him at Michigan after I did. I left. I was ashamed—"

Tessi cuts me off. "You don't have to explain yourself, Jules. I'd be lying if I didn't say it devastated me and that I spent hours worrying and crying. Your grandparents wouldn't give me your number. It destroyed all of us." She smiles gently, pausing between words. "But if you ever pull that stunt again, I'll never like you again and will more than likely hunt you down and cut off all your hair while you're sleeping."

I laugh, but something in her enlarged crazy eyes tells me she's not joking.

"Deal." I lean over, wrapping her up in a hug. "I love you, Tessi. I've missed you so much."

"Tell me everything on the drive over to the bar in the next town." She winks at me.

"Thank you."

I do as she instructed and fill her in on everything. From the pregnancy and birth of Whit and how Nana spent the first two months with me. The excuse she told everyone in town was a dear friend was in a sick state and had no one to take care of her. It wasn't too far from the truth.

Tessi interrupts every once in a while to fill me on her two births. Then it's all me rattling on mostly about Whit and how she developed so fast. I tell her about me barely graduating with an Associate's degree online. Then the tragic tale of attending beauty school that had an in-house daycare.

"Jesus, Jules, that's an amazing story. You know

the whole town was suspicious of your grandparents' monthly trips. They couldn't have done it without the help of—" She stops herself.

"Jessie," I finish. "Nana came clean about Jessie."

"Good. I was telling Brady that I feared the shit was really going to hit the fan and blow the roof off that farmhouse." Tessi puts her rig in park under the glow of the flickering bar lights. God, I've missed her off-the-wall humor and analogies.

"Brady?" I ask, snapping the seatbelt free and swiveling in the smooth leather seat to face her.

Her cheeks flush a hot pink. I drum my fingernails on the console, waiting for her to answer. "Brady's the baby daddy, the hubs, and the big D in my life."

"You're shitting me!" I slap at her. "Holy shit, Tessi, you two hated each other back in high school. Seriously, you couldn't stand to be around him."

"We fell in love." She shrugs.

We remain in the car for a good thirty minutes while Tessi fills me in on how Brady only finished a year of college, as did she. After one summer when they put aside their petty games and faux hatred for each other, sparks flew, and it's two kids later. Brady runs his dad's farm and helps out Jessie with his farm and custom farming business when he has time.

I inwardly flinch every time she speaks Jessie's name. I'm not sure I'll ever be able to not. Before the rush of nasty feelings flood in, I'm the first to jump from the car.

"Let's get drinking. God knows I can slam back

a few and be shit-faced." I waggle my eyebrows with my hand perched on the door.

Tessi leaps out her side, and we're striding to the neon lights of a dive bar. I could kiss Tessi on the lips for going to the next town over. Small towns are vicious. I guarantee at minimum that a week after my papa's funeral, all the town gossip, prying stares, and judgmental opinions will be zeroed in on me. My back will bear the bullseye target catching all the hate. I'll be the lying whore who left Jessie and never let him see his kid.

"Don't go there." Tessi jerks on my arm, throwing open the door to the bar.

"Uh?" I peer over to her.

"It may have been years we were separated, but girl, I can still read you like a book."

The blaring honkytonk music inside the bar cuts off all further discussion. The place is packed. Some garage-type band plays live music on top of the ramshackle stage. Old wood covers the walls as well as the floor. All of the planks are uneven, making me feel grateful I wore flat sandals. This is nothing like the few bars I went to back in California. Stark opposites. There's isn't one hoity-toity suit-wearing man to be seen.

Nope, it's a sea of worn denim, t-shirts, ball caps, and cowboy hats. Tessi grabs my hand, steering us to the bar. She saddles right up to it while I remain off to the side. I fear her arms are going to get splinters from the raw wood. Tin runs up the sides of it. Authentic and down-home as it gets.

"Tessi McCray, does your old man know you're

out on the town?" The bartender slings a rag over his shoulder.

A familiar dazzling smile and piercing blue eyes come into view. He recognizes me the moment I realize who he is. Cody Sterling. A classmate from high school, one of the band of brothers from the football glory days, and the biggest fuck boy to ever grace our little town. Teachers, mothers, aunts, and girls his age were all free game.

"Holy shit. Jules Jones, you've gotta be kidding me." He hops up on the bar and then glides right over. "You haven't aged a damn day."

Cody grabs me by the hips and tugs me to him. I throw my head back and laugh like a lunatic. His moves haven't changed a bit, and I'd bet his pick-up lines haven't either.

"Are you religious, Jules? Because hot damn, you're all the answers to my prayers." He wraps me in a tight hug and whispers in my ear. "Damn good to see you, old friend. So sorry to hear about your grandpa."

I find myself hugging him right back, relishing his embrace. "Thanks, Cody."

"Okay, okay. Enough, enough." Tessi breaks between the two of us. "Yes, she's single, Cody, but at least wait until after the funeral to put the full moves on her. Get your ass back behind the bar and make us some damn drinks."

He grumbles, swatting both of our asses, and leaps right back over the bar. I glance around, loving the fact nobody is staring with questioning looks. They're all about drinking, dancing, and more than likely finding a piece of tail for the night.

"What can I get you ladies?" Cody splays his palms on the bar top and waggles his eyebrows. "My cock is off the menu for the next three hours."

"You're disgusting." Tessi tosses a handful of peanuts at him. "Get us two shots of tequila to start with."

"You got it." Cody winks.

For the first time, since returning home, I feel light and a bit like the old Jules. Tonight is exactly what I needed. No doubt I'll be regretting the hell out of it in the morning. Then a thought strikes me.

"Tessi." I grab her arm, forcing her to focus on me. "Jessie was with Brady earlier today. Does that mean—"

She shakes her head, her blonde curls bouncing. "No, they're baling hay all night. We're good to go."

I relax back into the bar, thankful for that morsel of information. Jessie would indeed ruin tonight. Back in the day, I tended to be a mean drunk, especially when drinking tequila. It was either my inner bitch coming out to play or a sob fest. I decide on just one shot of tequila, then I'll drink beer.

"Here you go, ladies." Cody slides over two shot glasses. "Drinks are on me tonight."

"Thanks." I snag mine along with a lime wedge. "But we can pay."

"The owner thinks otherwise." He leans back on the counter behind him, crossing his arms over his chest.

"The owner?" I question.

"Didn't you see the name of the bar?" Tessi asks, perching her shot glass on her lips.

I shake my head. Cody points to the sign above his head. Cody's Shaggin' Shack, a motto clearly printed below in bold print. Drink, Laugh, and Fuck. A grin a mile wide spreads across my face. It had always been his dream. He proudly announced it at every career fair and even did his senior project on owning a bar. Good for him.

"Keep them coming, stud." Tessi clinks her shot glass to mine.

We cheer to the future and toss them back. The tequila burns all the way down to my belly; I forget the lime and salt, recoiling from the nasty taste. Tessi has another in my hand before I can opt for a beer.

"This is it for me." I hold up a hand.

"What?" Tessi squeals louder than the drumming of the band. "You wanted to get shit-faced."

"Tequila and I don't mix." I shake my head.

Cody slaps the bar from his leaning position. "I got you, girl."

He snags the tequila shot from my hand, and it's replaced with a bright red shot.

"What's this?" I ask, bringing it to my nose for a sniff. Smells like fruit punch.

"House special. We call it a Pussy Pleaser around these parts." He slaps his towel over his shoulder. "Your pussy will thank you later."

And with that, he's off slinging drinks for a line of customers that formed while we caught up.

"To getting your pussy pleased!" Tessi clinks her glass with mine.

I blush a bright red and shake my head. That is the absolute last thing on my mind. Tessi doesn't give me the chance to refuse. The sweet liquid glides down way smoother than the tequila. I smack my lips together and raise the shot glass over my head and wave it at Cody, who's down the bar. He gives me a nod, and before I know it a pitcher of the stuff slides down to us. We pound shots like they're going out of style.

We play around two-stepping and swinging each other as we finish off the pitcher and make some serious damage on the next. In the back of mind, I know this is very dangerous since it tastes like candy, but frankly, I don't give a damn.

The band is long gone with the speakers blaring a mix of music. My head swims in relaxation and comfort. I've missed my type of people. It's now that I realize I've been living in a foreign land and barely surviving thanks to my Whitty girl.

"Oh my God!" Tessi jerks me out to the center of the now-barren dance floor. The edges of my sandals catch on the uneven hardwood floor. "It's our jam. Our favorite mix-up of 90's songs from dance team."

Tessi holds out her hand counting down, and then it's on like Donkey Kong, or at least in my head it is. We pop our hips and kick out our legs all the while not missing a move with our arms. Once the mix-up ends, the bar erupts in cheers and catcalls.

I wipe my bangs back from my sweaty forehead to see Cody standing on the bar doing a slow clap. I press my fingers to my lips and send him an air kiss. Then a loud and old familiar jam begins blaring throughout the small bar.

Tessi and I scream the words out loud pumping our fists in the air as if we were seventeen year olds. I glance at the open garage door of the bar and let it all go. Tessi and I begin sliding and grinding our hips to "Tootsie Roll" by 69 Boyz. Massive hands grab my hips, and a hard body grinds up behind me. Cody and I rock out each move of the dance.

We don't stop grooving and jamming through "Cotton Eye Joe," "Don't Stop the Jam," and countless others. Cody keeps his hands on my hips and other various body parts. I don't mind. It's nice to have a man who I trust to have his hands and lips grazing my neck. I know it's all in good fun. It's just the way Cody is.

When "Push It" comes on, we get out of control. Cody acts out every part of the song, and I play along as a willing victim. The dance itself is provocative as hell, even turning on parts I haven't felt in years. It's our yelps of glee and laughter that make it all fun and games. Tessi joins in, sandwiching herself between us.

The music dies after "Push It," playing a Patsy Cline tune. It doesn't stop Cody. He grabs me, pulling me into a seductive slow dance. Tessi disappears. My head fogs with old memories and could have beens. I get lost in her thick, sultry voice without a care in the world.

It's not until the song ends that I learn why I should've alerted to why Tessi escaped the dance floor. When I glance over to the slivered-up bar, the picture becomes crystal clear. Jessie. Brady's flanked at his side with Tessi all up in his business. Hands are in places they shouldn't be in public. The two don't seem to mind at all. It's Jessie that causes my spine to stiffen. He's pissed off and so very fucking hot. His strong jawline clenches as his fists flex and straighten. His white work t-shirt is dirtied up from a hard day's work. I let my eyes flutter shut, knowing exactly how he'd feel, smell, and taste. Goosebumps break out on my skin. I want him, need him, even though I know for damn sure none of the above can ever happen. I don't want him. I repeat those simple four words over and over in my head.

It doesn't work. I want him so fucking bad. When he has the audacity to stomp out on the dance floor, all of those desired feelings disappear. Only anger and hatred remain. I see the man who had the balls to turn me away. Throw his unborn child and me away like a piece of trash. I hate him.

Chapter 5

Jessie

"Let's go home. I'm fucking exhausted." I slump back in Brady's truck.

My body isn't operating from a long day of work, but from everything else that's flooded back into my life. Whit's toothy grin and loving nature haunted me all day. The hate stemming from Jules directed right at me gutted me each pass of the tractor on the field.

We are supposed to be baling tonight. The thing about farming is that the best laid plans never happen. The baler broke down, and now we are off for the night. Even though I'm as exhausted as I am, I know for certain I won't be able to sleep a fucking wink. My girl is back in town. My biggest mistake. One I'd do all over again even if my pro career was legit. I'd give it up all for her. Knew the moment I stepped foot on the field for training camp in Michigan I wasn't me. I was fucked up. And now it's just not my girl in town—it's my girls in town.

"Tessi is out at Cody's. We are stopping by for a drink," Brady replies.

"Fuck," I growl, sinking back in the seat and pulling the brim of my ball cap over my eyes. "I'll wait in the truck. Not in the damn mood."

"Whatever floats your damn boat, man. I'm going to get Tessi. She hasn't been out with Jules since high school."

That last part gets my attention. I jolt straight up like a starving man for a piece of juicy t-bone.

"What was that?" I lean forward.

"Tessi took Jules out. Ran into her the other day and she said Jules wasn't doing too hot, and let's face it, Tessi has been gutted since the day Jules left." Brady turns into the parking lot for Cody's bar.

The place is damn packed. I groan, knowing it's a Friday night, more than likely the live band has just ended, and now it's a free-for-all drunken party. My first thought goes to Whit. I know I have no right to judge Jules and what she does with Whit. Can't lie, though, my chest tightens. I'd give anything to have that sweet little girl curled up next to me. I threw away that hope and dream years ago.

Before Brady swings open the door to the bar, he turns to me and presses a hand into my chest. "She's not yours anymore. Don't know what in the hell happened between you two. I could put the pieces together, but here's the thing—she's not yours, and you have no right to her."

With that, we waltz into the bar. The music is blaring like I knew it would be. I glance behind the bar to see Cody's employees busting their asses and slinging drinks. I could use one or ten right about now. We manage to make our way to the bar and order two whiskeys, neat. After we have our drinks, an opening at the bar splits wide open, and we take it.

Doesn't take very long for me to spot the action on the dance floor. Thank fuck I just slammed a drink and had a fresh one in my hand. Brady's advice rolls over and over in my head. I do my best to heed it. Each bitter swallow of whiskey does its job to dull the pain and simmer down the rage boiling inside of me.

Seeing Cody and Jules dance like they're long lost lovers does me in. When he thrusts his hips up into her ass and fist pumps the air, I'm a goner. I no longer see red; it's more like sheer unholy and unleashed rage. I'm going to snap his motherfucking neck. Jules isn't mine, and Brady nailed that on the head. Doesn't mean my mind processed it.

I slam the rest of my drink and stomp out on the dance floor. My hand clutches Jules' upper arm like the other day. A startled gasp escapes her. She hiccups and then giggles. She's drunk off her ass.

When Jules tugs away from me, I'm forced to clench my fists and let her walk away like I did so many years ago. It was my biggest mistake, and it seems it's all I'm good at. Her and Cody saddle back up to the bar chugging some red shit. I keep an eye on her while keeping my distance. Cody has always been a close friend, but when his lips land on hers and Jules clings to his neck, I'm done. Long fucking overcooked. I don't stop this time.

"Jules," I growl at her back.

She whirls around. "Jessie. Oh my God, it's freaking Jessie, the local stud."

Her high-pitched squeal draws the attention of the entire bar. The music has been turned down, and now all eyes are on us. This bar may be in the next town over, but there are several familiar faces. I'm about to bat down a hornet's nest with a twig and don't give a single damn.

"It's time to go," I say in a smooth voice.

"Oh, what? Jessie wants something, I guess he takes care of it." She drags out the five words, and they drip in venom and pain.

"Not here, Jules."

She thumps a finger in my chest. "Fuck you, Jessie James."

Tessi interrupts her. "That's the Cher song."

Jules doesn't stop. "Fuck you, Jessie, you broke my heart. No, not only did you break my heart, you ruined it. I came to you telling you I was pregnant, and you dumped me like a rotten fish! You blocked me out like a pompous, self-serving dickhead, so you don't have a right to say two words to me."

She whirls around with her arms raised in the air. "You all heard it! Spread it back to Boone. Jessie and I have a child. She's not his, though, because he wanted nothing to do with her." Her voice cracks, and the tears spill over. "I'm back because the guy I called my dad died. I was forced from this town, and now I'm only back to lay his dead body in the ground. If one of you pathetic fuckers dares speaks ill of my daughter, we'll have words."

I know she's not done with her rampage. It's her

uncontrollable sobbing that stops her. She doesn't have any other choice than to collapse into my chest. Instinct takes over, and I hold her. Don't like one fucking bit that the attention of the bar is focused on us. I lift her up into me; her legs wrap around my waist as my hands clutch her ass. It's natural, and this is home.

I jerk my chin to Brady. Tessi and he follow me out the door. I had two whiskeys, far from being drunk considering I could polish off a fifth of Crown Royal each night and still function. It's what my life has come to. Brady tosses me his keys. I give him a jerk of the chin, striding to his truck.

"Don't let me go," Jules manages to get out between sobs.

I change my course and make my way to the passenger seat. I climb in, keeping Jules clutched to my front. We remain in the parking lot, sitting and not exchanging a word. I don't move, letting her release everything she's kept bottled up for years. It's not a breakthrough with us but a baby step.

Jules' cries cease. Her body goes still, and I know she's passed out. I don't move. I kiss the top of her head and keep her clutched to my front for minutes that turn into hours. When the sun threatens to rise, I know it's time to take her home.

I move with ease, laying her across the bench seat and cradling her head in my lap as I drive. I don't waste a second soaking everything about Jules in. Her emerald green eyes that pulled me in from kindergarten. Her wild antics and carefree personality that stole my heart right down to her out of control laughter. I remember it all. They're the same things that have haunted my dreams.

Her childhood home is silent when I carry her in, her light snores the only thing filling the space. It reminds me of the times we'd sneak out to the barn and spend the night together. We'd both hustle our asses home before the roosters crowed.

Jane and my sweet Whit are cuddled up in Jules' bed. I sneak back down to the living room and place Jules on the couch. She reaches up for me, snagging my t-shirt. She pulls me down to her.

"I never stopped loving you, and I hate you for that, Jessie."

Her features slacken back to sleep. It's a slice of hope and a dagger to the heart at the same time. After getting her bundled in blankets and her sandals wrestled off her feet, I creep back up to her bedroom and study Whit. God, that little girl has the ability to destroy me.

Her features are miniature versions of Jules. She's the light in the darkness. Everything that's good. I swipe back her hair from her face and see she's sleeping in one of my old high school shirts with a worn teddy clutched to her chest.

It's in this moment I know beyond anything certain that I'll fight with everything to have this little girl in my life, even if it crushes Jules.

Chapter 6

Jules

"She's not dead, Nana."

"She's probably going to wish she was," she replies.

I don't even have the energy to groan. My throat is drier than hell. My head pounds and my stomach lurches with just the thought of waking up.

"What does that mean, Nana?" Whit asks.

"It just means your momma stayed up way too late and missed her bedtime."

"I get the mean, mean Momma face that makes me scared when I do that."

More rattling ensues with whatever the two are doing.

"You'll understand one day, lil' pumpkin. It's not easy being a momma."

"Yeah."

I can only picture my sweet Whit shrugging.

"But is it bacon time?"

Nana's soft laughter echoes around the house.

"Yes, it is."

The racket from the kitchen ricochets in my skull. My throat coats in dryness. It's like the fucking Mojave Desert. I'm dying. I swear I'm two seconds away from death's bed. I enter the state of being both exhausted and wide awake while the marching drum continues to beat out a steady rhythm in my head. My stomach decides to join in, tumbling and swirling around.

Bathroom. I race upstairs just in time to pray to the porcelain gods then experience the worst case of whiskey shits. By the time Satan has exited my body, I'm done with the day, even though it's barely eight in the morning. I collapse down on my bed, not once worried about what's surrounding me. I nestle my cheek in my pink pillow, inhaling Whit's innocent scent, and drift off to sleep, not one single thought on my mind.

Giggles. Loud and genuine giggles break through my foggy haze as I stretch my arms above my head and gain my bearings. Yep, my head still swims and is murky as hell. I am never drinking again. Famous last words, I know, but still never tying on a knot like that one for a long, long damn time.

I kick my legs over the bed. It takes several seconds for my body to kick in gear with what I'm hearing. On steady legs, I walk over to the window. I blink several times. The blinding light pierces through the crystal-clear glass. My heart seizes in my chest when the picture develops before me. It's one I've dreamed of and feared at the same time.

My fingertips go on autopilot, lifting up the old

style paned window. The fresh breeze strikes across my flesh. It's everything. I focus in on Whit prancing behind Jessie, who's moving hand lines. Irrigating is a merciless game that must go on to make everything bountiful.

His attention is on packing the pipe to the next area of pasture. Whit doesn't pick up on the fact he's concentrating as she rattles on.

"So about the dance studio? Did you sign me up?"

Jessie tosses down the pipe and rolls up the sprinklers. He peers over to her and nods. It's not a firm answer. Whit takes it as one.

"So, should I wear a purple or pink tutu? Will the girls like me? Do you think I'll be the best dancer?"

Whit's questions trail Jessie as he strides to the end of the alfalfa hay to the main line. He jerks his head, giving Whit non-committal answers.

"Honey." Hands land on the tops of my shoulders. "You have to address that. She's been magnetized to Jessie."

I remain silent. Even with the hangover, anger and hatred pour through. I'll never forget those words Jessie so carelessly tossed at me. No matter how much I love him. Spoken words always leave an imprint. I'll never forget them.

"She loves him," Nana goes on. "It was an immediate bond between those two. You know the months we visited you, your papa and I saw Jessie in Whit. She walked before she should've via the books and doctors. She was speaking full sentences at one, ready to control the world. It was Jessie's drive."

Her fingertips dig into the tops of my shoulders, cementing her message. I've known it since Whit was born. Jessie's ghost has taunted me around every corner. Her smile, her drive, and her giggle were all 'reminders of my greatest love. I never stopped loving that man, no matter how hard I fought to.

I nod, acknowledging Nana's words. It's time, and I for one know it's long overdue. As Jessie walks back up the pipes to a clogged sprinkler, Whit prances behind him. He reaches back into his worn jeans, pulling out pliers. He works on it as Whit studies his every move. Soon enough, water spurts out. He doesn't have the valve on the main line turned all the way on. Jessie gets distracted with his phone.

His hand moves across the screen. I don't even want to think about who he is texting. I have no idea if he's married or has a loved one waiting on him. The thought threatens to make me sick once again.

Whit grows bored. Naturally, she begins playing with the sprinkler while Jessie goes from texting to answering a phone call. His jaw tightens and shoulders go taut. Whoever he's talking to, it's not a pretty conversation. He punches his phone then slams it in his back pocket.

Whit isn't detoured, her front already soaked from the sprinkler. Jessie kneels down to whisper something to her. The pressure heightens, and she flicks the sprinkler right at his face. Dead-on bullseye. It takes Jessie moments to realize what she's just done.

I wait with baited breath to see his reaction. Nana walked away from behind me moments ago. Jessie peers down at his soaked shirt then back to Whit, who has the sprinkler aimed on him. She's relentless in her efforts.

Jessie doesn't flinch or even react. Whit stands there, soaking the shit out of him. Her cries of laughter echo up to my room. Everything happens so fast. Jessie swoops down, grabbing our daughter in his arms. She giggles and laughs until the sprinkler is aimed on her. He soaks the ever-loving shit out of her.

Their bodies become a blur as they whirl around in the sprinklers, carefree and happy as can be. I wipe away a stray tear, watching them as my head continues to pound, and I feel like my body has been run over by a Mack truck. Jessie swoops Whit in his arms and hoists her up on his shoulders.

"So what about that dance class?" Whit's hands grip the top of Jessie's head as she leans forward, peering down at him.

They now stand in the yard on the side of the house, making it easy to hear their conversation, clear as day.

"Whit," Jessie's stature visibly droops, "things are complicated. Your momma isn't my biggest fan, but I will talk to her."

"She probably thinks you're a douche just like Aunty Lydia thinks Roman is."

I slap my hand over my mouth, hiding my smile and stifling my laughter. I swear that girl will never have a filter.

"A douche?" Jessie cranes his neck to look at

her. "And who in the hell is Roman?"

"Momma's boyfriend and my aunt Lydia calls him a douche, douche bag, or douche canoe."

"Your mom has a boyfriend?" he growls.

"Yep, and between us, he's a douche."

"Sounds like it." Jessie glances up to the window.

I don't move. I can't. I stare back down at him. My hand runs down the windowpane. I'm so damn confused right now. Nana is right. We have to talk. Figure shit out because it's clear Jessie loves Whit and deserves the chance to get to know her. There's no doubt at all in my mind that Whit is hopelessly and madly in love with Jessie. Just like her momma.

I force myself into a hot shower even though the only thing I want to do is curl up and hide under my blankets for the rest of the day. My heart remains shattered. The fragments of the once-perfect organ ache in pain for so many different reasons. Silent tears cascade with the shower water. I'm left even more exhausted after drying off. I firmly put on my mask for the day and head downstairs. I have to be the strong one.

The one thing I have missed about this small town is being able to dress in comfy clothes and not getting a sideways glance. Back in California, I'd get glares from other parents dropping Whit off at preschool in yoga pants and a hoodie. My bare feet slap down on the wood steps. I slide on a pair of worn and well-loved flip-flops once I'm at the bottom of the steps and tug down my shorts.

"Ssshhh," Whit holds her finger up to her lips, "I'm not 'pose to get into the brownies until after dinner."

"Well, maybe you should wait," Jessie suggests, stepping back and running his hands through his hair.

It's now that I notice Whit is wearing his snapback on her head, backward. She shrugs, thinking about it for a few moments, before her tiny hand dives into the bag. She's no dummy, offering Jessie one and insisting he take it. I know exactly what her train of thought is—if she's going to get busted, Whit plans to take him down with her.

I wait until they've both taken several bites out of the brownies then clear my throat. Both of their heads whip in my direction. Whit goes on autopilot mode to save her butt.

"Momma, you look so beautiful." She tucks the brownie behind her back.

Jessie's shoulders grow tight, and he takes a step back the closer I get.

"Whit." I point at her.

"You really do, Momma. I love you." She sways side to side with both hands tucked behind her back.

I move fast, grabbing the half-eaten brownie from her and shoving it in my mouth. I lean down and kiss her cheek. A masculine scent that's full of hard work, sweat, and fucking Jessie assaults me. It ignites parts of me that shouldn't be paying a bit of attention.

"Good try, little one. Now you won't get one with dinner."

"Momma!" Her eyes go wide.

When I don't back down from my stance, her eyes grow watery, her bottom lip pops out, and the water works begin.

"Whit." I kneel down. "You knew you weren't supposed to get into those, and you chose to anyway. This is a natural consequence."

"Jessie had one, too." She points at him and barely gets the words out between sobs.

"Well, he won't be having any for dinner either," I reply. Her cries grow louder. "Go on up to our room until you can calm down."

She stomps her foot and turns on Jessie. "Thanks a lot for sticking up for me."

Before she manages to make it all the way to the stairs, Jessie stops her and gives her the rest of his brownie and a long hug.

"Will you take me up there?" Whit's voice quavers.

Jessie turns to look at me, waiting for approval. He pulls her to his chest, and Whit lays her head down on his shoulder, continuing to cry. A piece of the anger I've held for years dissipates when he begins whispering in her ear and patting her back.

I sink back on the counter, grateful there's still coffee around. I pour myself a cup, adding plenty of creamer. Jessie comes back down several minutes later.

"Coffee?" I ask, holding out a mug. It's an olive branch. I have to be civil with him.

"Sure." He nods, tucking his hands in his pockets.

I don't have to ask how he drinks it. I know. I know everything about the tall, sexy as hell man standing in the kitchen way too close to me.

"She's adjusting to the change. Whit doesn't

typically throw that big of a fit. She gets busted a lot doing things she's been told not to. I'm certain she's exhausted, overwhelmed, and confused." I turn around, holding out his mug, to find Jessie mere feet from me.

I step back only to have the edge of the counter bite into the bottom of my back. He doesn't make a move to back up. Those whiskey-colored eyes soak me up. He doesn't have to say a word. Everything is conveyed in his stare.

"You're fucking beautiful, Jules. I know I don't have the right to tell you that, but it's eating me up on the inside."

My hands tremble. I stretch it out, offering the coffee. Jessie's fingers brush with mine as he grips the mug. He doesn't make a move to pull away.

"We need to talk," I whisper.

"We do." He grabs my hand, lacing our fingers together, and guides us to the dining room table. He goes back for my mug of coffee.

"Want any coffee with your creamer?" He sets down the mug and smirks.

I shake my head, gripping the sides of the mug. The pounding in my head escalates.

"Not feeling so hot?" he asks.

"Is it that evident?" I shrug.

"Yeah, can tell you're dying of pain."

"Damn Cody. I'm never drinking again. I swear." I blow on my coffee and take a light sip. "I don't drink often, Jessie, just so you know. It's usually a few glasses of wine after Whit goes down."

"Stop." He reaches over, placing his hand on

mine, squeezing it gently. "You're an amazing mom. I will never judge anything you've done. Ever. So let's not even bring up that topic again."

I nod. "She deserves to know. We need to tell her."

"What does she know about her dad?" He keeps our hands connected. In an odd way, it gives me strength to carry on. None of it makes sense. I'm thankful beyond words we are having open communication.

"She only recently started asking questions because of daddy-daughter functions at her school." I swallow hard and close my eyes. "Every single time she's asked about you, I've told her you were a very busy guy and had to move but that you loved her very much. She sleeps in your old football t-shirt. It's her favorite."

"I do love her. Fell in love the moment I saw her, Jules." He clears his throat. "I don't deserve any of this. I can never tell you how thankful I am for giving this to me. I can't take back what I did. I've regretted it every single day."

"Since your injury, right?" I can't help the snarky dig. I'm trying here. I really am.

He shakes his head. "No, since the moment you walked away from me in the gymnasium."

I nod and pull my hand back. This is all becoming too real and in my face. "I'd like to be there when you tell her."

"Yes, I'll need you there." He leans back in the chair, massaging tension out of the back of his neck. "This dance thing. She keeps asking about it."

"You can do that with her."

"How long are you guys staying, Jules? When are you going back?"

It's not lost on me he doesn't use the word "home." California isn't my home and never will be.

"I don't know. I work from home. After the funeral, Nana is going to need all the support she can get. I'm playing it from day to day."

"That's fair." He snaps his mouth shut. Whatever he was going to say dies on his lips. "I'll be back for dinner tonight, and we can go from there."

Jessie tilts back his coffee mug, draining the rest of the coffee. He stands and leaves without another word.

Chapter 7

Jessie

I take my hat off and hold it in front of me when entering the funeral home. Cars line both sides of the road. The place is packed for the viewing. A floral scent intoxicates me. There are dozens and dozens of bouquets. I spot the one I sent over. I know it's mine because of the different shades of purple. One color. Jules' favorite.

It takes me long moments before I spot Jules standing next to her grandma. She's dressed in a simple off-the-shoulder black dress and standing tall and proud, nodding her head listening to whatever is being said. My gaze roams down her exposed tanned legs. I can't get enough of her. And it's not because I'll never have her again. Hell no, it's true love. The kind that never fades or dies out no matter the amount of years that have gone by.

A twirling motion catches my attention. Whit is snuggled up to her mom's leg, swinging the bottom of her black dress. Her tiny hands have black gloves on them. Her hair is piled up on her head and tied off with a black headband. When she raises her head, bright red lipstick comes into view. I can't help the smile that plays out on my face. She's the sunshine in this storm.

I find myself walking over to them. Whit's eyes grow in size when she spots me. She drops her mom's hand and bolts for me. I bend down, catching her in my arms. Her tiny arms wrap around my neck.

"Oh, Jessie, I'm so glad you're here."

I stand up, keeping her tucked to my chest. "Yeah?"

"I hate it here."

"I know, baby girl. I know." I kiss her head.

"Momma and Nana are so sad, and these people won't shut up."

I chuckle. "Oh Whit, you never sugarcoat a thing."

I step over to Jules' side. She peers up at me with a small smile. Without thinking, I lean down and kiss her forehead.

"Jules, I'm so sorry."

"Thank you," she whispers.

It's not lost on me she hasn't stepped away from me or reacted to the kiss. It was natural as if we haven't missed a single day.

"Can we go, Momma?" Whit runs her hand through the hair on the nape of my neck.

"No, honey. Soon, though."

She huffs.

I lean back down in a selfish move to whisper into Jules' ear. Her lilac scent washes over me. My lips glide along the shell of her ear. I have no self-control right now.

"I can take her by the dance studio and introduce her to the teacher, then head home," I offer.

Jules shakes her head. Her sad eyes stare back up at me. "What if someone says something?"

"They won't," I reassure her.

After several long moments, she finally nods. "Okay, thank you. I have a meatloaf at home for dinner tonight."

"Yuck. I hate meatloaf," Whit whines.

"Hey." I tap her nose. "We'll figure out something. You've gotta be a good girl, okay?"

She nods her head. Jules grabs my forearm, tugging me closer to her. She shocks the shit out of me when she reaches up on her tiptoes and kisses my cheek.

"Thank you, Jessie."

The greedy bastard that I am steals one more kiss. It's the sweetest hell pulling my lips from her forehead. I weave through the crowd, ignoring all the inquisitive stares. Shit like that in this small town has always driven me fucking nuts. It wore on me after I returned home injured. It was as if I had to prove myself again. I played right into the head games. Not now. There are two important ladies in my life, and they're all that matter.

"Jessie." Whit taps my cheek. "I need my booster seat from Momma's car."

She points to Jules' car the same time I hear my name being hollered. I turn around to see Jules jogging down the steps, waving her keys in the air.

"You can take my car." She extends the keys,

breathing heavily.

"No way in hell am I driving that thing," I reply.

She rolls her eyes. "Jessie, it's a car."

"Exactly." I snag the keys from her hand and grab the booster seat while juggling Whit.

"See, problem fixed." I hand her back the keys.

Underneath the sunshine, I can see through Jules' light layer of make-up. The black lines under her eyes are evident. Not to mention her sagging shoulders.

"You doing okay?" I brush away a stray piece of hair.

"Needed a break from in there." She brushes her palms down her front. "It's almost over."

Jules take a few moments gaining her bearings before kissing Whit and walking back into the funeral home. Whit shows me how to put her seat in my truck. It's not rocket science, but I listen attentively to each of her instructions. I don't know much about kids, but I do know airbags are a big no-no as well having little kids sit in the front. Thank God this old gem doesn't have any airbags or I wouldn't be able to take my daughter anywhere. I make a note to buy a booster seat to have in my truck.

"Um, Jessie, you're forgetting something." Whit points when I settle in behind the steering wheel.

I quirk up an eyebrow in question.

"Seat belt." She rolls her eyes.

I crack a smile and follow the little queen's orders. The cab doesn't stay quiet for long as I pull out on Main Street.

"Jessie?"

"Yeah."

"Do you think my papa is in heaven?" She stares out the window.

"I sure do. There's no doubt." I reach over and grab her petite hand. "He was one of the best guys I ever knew."

"Does he just sit up there on the clouds? It makes me sad he's so far away from all of us."

I gently squeeze her hand the same time a vice crushes my heart. "Naw, he's up there with all of his friends and animals that have passed. He's never too far away. He has the perfect seat up there watching everything you do, that's for certain."

"Okay." She bobs her head.

I pull in front of the dance studio on the edge of town. My phone goes off in my pocket. The inevitable call I knew was coming. Shocked as shit it hadn't happened yet. I haven't had time to take care of it. I reach in my pocket, sending it straight to voicemail.

"Who was that, Jessie?" Whit keeps her head down, struggling with the buckle on the seatbelt.

"No one important." The words are bitter rolling off my tongue. It's a harsh statement, but the truth. Shayna was nothing but a time filler. The next step in life and all that jazz. Settling is an understatement in this situation. In the beginning, I thought there was a good chance it would all work out. I should've trusted my gut. Shayna loves the glory of being with the once hometown hero and head football coach. She gloats on the glory and lives it up.

Whit scrambles out of her booster seat and into

my lap. We wiggle out of the truck. She takes my hand and begins swinging it as we walk up to the dance studio.

"You know I really love it here. It's so much better than California."

"You have no idea how happy that makes me."

Forty minutes later, Whit is signed up for hip-hop and ballet. Her grin is contagious. I was shocked how shy she was around other kids her age. It took her a bit to warm up, and once she did, it was all over. With her schedule clutched to her chest, she skips to the truck.

"Tuesday, don't forget, Jessie. You have to take me, okay?"

"It's a date, sweetie." I kiss the top of her head and round the front of my truck. "How about pizza for dinner?"

"Yes, yes, yes!" She fist-pumps the air. "This is the best day ever."

Nerves of fear and anxiety course through me. God, I hope she'll be thinking that later tonight after dinner. The events of the day settle in on me. I'm bone tired and only riding the high of being around Whit and Jules.

Chapter 8

Jules

"Doing okay?" Tessi wraps an arm around my shoulders. "What can I get you?"

"I'd say wine and a bed, but I'll just go with a bed tonight." I sag into her.

"The turnout was amazing. How's your grandma holding up?"

I shake my head. "She's putting on a front. I'm waiting for her to crash. It's going to be brutal."

"I know. I'll be by your side, and honestly, you and Whit are exactly what she needs. Speaking of Whit, I saw Jessie come in earlier."

She leaves the statement open, waiting on details. If I had the energy to be pissed, I would be. The moment I made eye contact with him, I felt safe and as if I could make it through this living nightmare. His starched Wranglers hugged his ass perfectly. It was his button-down shirt with the few top buttons undone that did me in. The sight, scent, and touch made everything better.

"Yeah, he took Whit to the dance studio. This has been hard as hell on her. She's resilient but acting out a bit."

"God, the way he looks at her and you. It's something else, but I'm surprised Shayna wasn't by his side."

This gets my attention. I pop up in a standing position. "Shayna?"

"Yeah, they've been together for a while now." Tessi's face softens in remorse.

"As in Shayna Morten? As in the bitch who made it her life's mission to make my life a living hell?"

She nods and nibbles down on her bottom lip. "I'm sorry, Jules."

I wave her off. "It doesn't matter."

The biggest lie that has ever left my lips. I'm not stupid, knowing damn well there have been other women in Jessie's life, but Shayna? Looks like she won in the long end. Anger brews up low in my belly. I see red. I have no idea why I'm feeling this way, and it only pisses me off even more. A tiny voice in the back of my head whispers the truth…*because you're still in love with him.*

"A few nights ago, her cousin proposed to one of her friends at Gravy Dave's. The word on the street is she flipped out on Jessie, making a whole scene. He settled with her. He doesn't love her."

I hold up a hand. "None of my business. Seriously, I have enough shit to work through. I have to focus on Whit and my grandma."

"Okay, okay." She wraps me up in a hug. "I'm sorry about all of this. Are you sure you don't want that wine?"

I grumble. "I seriously think I'm still hung-over, so that's a big fat no. Thank you for being here, Tessi."

Once the final person leaves the viewing, Grandma and I walk out to my car hand in hand.

"That was the worst thing I've ever had to do." She stops walking and breaks down. "How am I going to do this?"

I drop her hand and tuck her head to my shoulder, letting her cry. This is her rock bottom. Never in all of the years has she broken down in public, let alone on Main Street. I give her time before getting her settled in the car.

"Jessie and Whit are meeting us at home." I break the silence first.

"She loves him. Makes my heart happy," she replies.

"He's with Shayna." The statement comes out before I can think it over.

Nana clutches her purse in her lap. "He is. No one can stand her. Much hasn't changed. Jessie is miserable with her."

She goes on to tell me about the latest gossip and proposal disaster. It turns out it was the night I drove back into town and the reason Gravy Dave's was packed. It's enough information to make me sick. My heart races in my chest, and sweat beads form on my forehead. The thought of Jessie proposing to another woman, let alone Shayna, devastates me. Then a vicious cycle of hating and hurting begins.

"Jules." Nana reaches over and grabs my hand. I

keep my vision steady on the road. "What Jessie did was wrong. Nobody will ever question that. He was young and dumb and caught up in the moment. He destroyed you, but you kept pushing on, and now you have an amazing little girl."

"Nana, don't—" I try to cut her off.

"You need to hear this." She squeezes my hand. "Jessie came home destroyed, and it wasn't because of his knee injury. It was you. He begged Papa for information on you. He never cracked. Jessie stopped asking the day Papa laid his ass out in the barn and gave him a real ass chewing. From that moment on, Jessie came by to help us out, kept his head down, and never asked another question. He's never been the same."

I pull into my parking space in front of the house. The porch lights glow in the dusk of the evening. Jessie and Whit both sit cross-legged facing each other with a deck of cards between them. Whit slaps Jessie's hand when he reaches for a card in the deck.

"Well, neither have I." I slam my hand on the steering wheel. "Whit has been my priority. I've had a handful of dates and only two relationships I thought could go somewhere. It was all put on the back burner while he was here fucking Shayna and still being the hometown hero now as the head winning football coach. It hurts, and that pisses me off. I don't want it to hurt, and it's killing me."

"Jules, he's hurting, too. The moment you came back into town, everything changed for the both of you. All I can tell you is that you have two choices here, baby girl. You can stay pissed off and bitter or find peace somewhere in all of this. And to me, the peace is easy when you watch those two together. Dig deep and let go of the past. Your grandpa pissed me off so many times. I'd react, slam doors, ignore him, and cuss his ass out. It wasn't worth it. None of it was. I'd give anything to have just one more day with him."

With that, she opens the door and walks up the sidewalk. Whit bounds off the porch, rushing to Nana and hugging the hell out of her. Jessie stands to his feet, stretching out his back, and then rests his hands on his hip. His gaze goes straight to me. My heart sinks to my toes knowing the conversation that's going to take place tonight. I have to be honest with him even though it will leave me in a vulnerable and nasty place. I've guarded my heart for years, and now it's time to peel away that shield.

"Momma." Whit races up to me, meeting me at the gate with her arms raised in the air. I scoop her up. "I'm in dance! And we got pizza for dinner. Jessie knew your favorite kind without me telling him. He knows you like pepperoni and jalapenos."

She twists up her face. That combination has always disgusted her.

"Sounds good." I kiss her cheek and walk the rest of the way up the sidewalk.

"And look!" She points to the table on the porch. "We set the table."

Flickering candles come into view, and I laugh. Whit has been obsessed with romantic dinners for months now after watching princess movies. Paper plates frame the table with a dandelion in the center of each. A bottle of white wine sits on the table, a beer in front of one plate, and a tall glass of milk in front of another plate. My stomach doesn't roll at the sight of the wine. I'm excited to see it. The hangover from hell finally has relented.

Whit ushers each of us in our spot, proud as hell at the setup.

"Joe Dandy still makes pizza?" I ask, taking a huge bite out of the slice. I groan through the mouthful of mozzarella cheese and tangy pizza sauce. "Still the best ever."

"Sure does." Nana cuts a piece of her pizza off. "Their son took it over a few years back and didn't change a thing."

Whit devours her slice of cheese pizza then makes me proud when she digs into a green salad next to her.

"Still eat that nasty pizza." I point my slice over to Jessie. "I'll never understand how anyone thinks it's okay to put pineapple on pizza."

He smirks. "The only kind I eat."

Whit rattles on about her dance class. Her enthusiasm is well needed. Nana stands from her spot, kisses Whit on top of the head, and excuses herself for bed. When I go to follow her to make sure she's okay, she pushes me away. I let her go because I know all too well how much silence and some alone time is needed right now.

I sit back down to find Whit looking between Jessie and me. It's as if she knows what's coming and just waiting for one of us to speak up. Jessie shows no signs of talking, so I take charge, needing this to be over.

"Come here, Whitty girl." I pat my lap. She

wastes no time climbing into it. I run my hands through her silky curls and kiss the top of her head. "Jessie and I have something we want to talk to you about."

"Yes!" She clutches her hands to her chest. "I knew it. You guys are getting married, buying me a pony, and we are living here forever."

Jessie chokes on the swallow of his beer. I shake my head and smile. I'm thinking Whit is going to take this news like a champ. At least that's the hope I'm clinging to.

"Not quite." I shuffle her around in my lap so she's facing me. Jessie drags his chair to our side of the table. It's the first time he's been by my side while dealing with our little girl.

"Then what is it?" She cranes her neck, flicking her lip with her index finger.

Jessie clears his throat. I give him time. In these moments, my nerves amp up. I sound like a broken record, but this is something I never thought I'd have to face.

"Whit." He reaches over, taking her hand. "You know your momma grew up in this house and town, right?"

She nods her head. "She was the homecoming queen. I want to be that when I grow up and have a dress. Jessie, will you buy me a dress?"

A crooked smirk appears on his face. "Of course, but stay with me here on this, okay? Your momma and I were best friends growing up since we were able to walk. She was my favorite person." He pauses. "She's still one of my favorite people. We fell in love and were high school sweethearts. I've never loved anyone like her until I met you, and then there was room in my heart for two endless loves."

"Okay-y-y…" Whit draws out with her eyebrows scrunched up in confusion.

I lay my hand on the top of Jessie's thigh, giving it an encouraging squeeze.

"I'm your dad, Whit." Tears brim in the corner of his eyes. "I'm your dad."

Silence sits thickly on all of our chests while Whit processes his words. She glances at me then back to Jessie.

"You are?" she whispers.

"Yes, Whit. God, I love you so much." He caresses her cheek.

"Are you still busy?" she asks, her lower lip trembling.

"Honey." I rub my hand up and down her back.

Jessie doesn't let me finish. "No, I'm not busy anymore, and you know what, Whit? I never should've been busy in the first place. It's the biggest regret of my life. And now that you're here, I'll never be busy again."

Whit bursts into tears and buries her face in my chest. I let her process everything, rubbing my hand in rhythmic, soothing circles on her back.

"This is a good thing," I whisper into the top of her head. "Your daddy is here and loves you. You get one more important person in your life."

She nods. Her voice comes out muffled as she speaks into the front of my dress. "I'm just scared I won't be good enough for Jessie to like me now. If he gets busy again—"

Jessie holds out his hands, and I let him take her. She burrows into his chest. "I'll never be too busy again, Whit. When you get older, I'll explain everything. I promise from the bottom of my heart that I'll never leave your side again. I love you, Whit, and I love your mom. I'm all yours."

He rocks her back and forth for long moments. Whit reaches over, searching for my hand. I hold it as Jessie rocks her to sleep. His cheek rests on the top of her head.

"That hurt," he finally mutters.

"She's confused and exhausted."

"Jules." He makes eye contact with me. "I'm struggling here. I'm not going to lie. I never thought this day would come. I know there's no way to erase my past mistake, but I'll do anything to make it right."

"All you have to do is love your little girl and be by her side, Jessie."

He nods. "What about us?"

"I heard about Shayna tonight. Doesn't seem there can be an us, and maybe it's for the best."

He winces. "I don't love her. Never have. It's pathetic, but I got tired of everyone harassing me about getting married and moving on."

"With her?" Bitterness creeps up in the back of my throat. "That was the final nail in the coffin, Jessie. After everything."

"I get it. All I'm asking for is a chance. Don't shut me out, Jules. I know that's asking a lot, but I'm sitting here begging just for a chance."

"Since we've been pretty damn good about ripping back the layers, I need to let you know that even through the devastation and life changes, I never quit loving you, Jessie."

It happens so fast I don't react. Hell, I wouldn't have even if I saw it coming. Jessie leans over, brushing his lips against mine one, two, three times before kissing me. My hands go up to cup his cheek. My fingers run along his scruff of his beard. His tongue sweeps across the seam of my lips, and I melt, opening for him. We face so many obstacles that could take us down forever, but this simple kiss makes everything right in the world for just a few seconds.

He pulls back, dropping his forehead to mine, keeping Whit clutched to his chest. "I just need one chance, Jules, just one."

I nod, not giving him a definite answer. By no means is my past free and clear of mistakes and sins. There are plenty of things people could use to judge me. I'm home. Whit is cuddled in her dad's arms, who happens to be the man I never fell out of love with.

Jessie's cellphone clatters on the tabletop. The shrill ringtone blares in the evening air. He reaches over to silence it before it wakes Whit, but not before I see a selfie of him and Shayna taunting me from the screen. Things change. Sometimes you can never go back, and that might have been the wake-up call I needed.

Chapter 9

Jessie

The roughest fucking night of my life. I barely slept an hour, wanting nothing more than to have Jules and Whit cuddled up to me. I'm going to need all the patience I can muster not to screw this up. It's so complicated and simple at the same time. I want my girls.

As I expected, Shayna was on my doorstep when I pulled my old truck into my driveway. She was red hot pissed—she'd already heard what's going on. I wouldn't expect anything less in a small town. She was so centered in her fit of rage she didn't even shed one single tear. It cemented the fact she never loved me because this didn't hurt her. She was only chasing a diamond ring with me.

The last six words she spewed my way before stomping down the sidewalk pissed me off because I know she'll make good on her promise.

"You're going to regret this, Jessie. I'll destroy you and your future."

The sneer on Shayna's face and the venom lacing her voice will never leave my memory. I'll protect my family from her. I will because Jules and Whit are mine. I wasn't invited to show up at Jules' home this morning. And I can't find two reasons to even care about it. I've been by Jack's side the last four years. He knocked me on my ass and put me in my place, letting me know I had no right to Jules. I took it like a man. Always respected him. The day his death was announced tore me apart. I swear I'll do him proud.

I shake my head. The ornery bastard upped the ante by not telling me about Whit. He always did have to get the last word in. The joke is on me. Best punchline ever. A beautiful one, equivalent to the sunset and all that other cheesy shit. Hell, I don't know what I'm talking about. All I do know is they are my life, and I can never thank Jack enough for giving them to me. That's why I'm here today. Not even earth's greatest disaster could devour me.

I'm here for my girls.

The front door to Jules' childhood home bursts open with a flash and whirl of black dashing down the steps.

"Jessie!" Whit pumps her arms as fast and hard as she can until she collides with me. "You came back."

I kneel down and bring her to my chest and kiss the top of her head. "I'll always come back. Never leaving you, little one."

"I'm so happy." She squeezes my neck.

"Where's your momma and Nana?" I stand up, beginning to walk slowly, soaking in each second of this tender moment.

"Momma is getting ready, and Nana is making a list in the kitchen." She pops her head up getting right in my face. "We have some bacon left over. Want some?"

"Duh!" I roll my eyes, earning an eye roll from Whit in return.

Whit wiggles out of my arms, rushing around to fetch a plate as soon as we enter the kitchen. She slides the remainder of the bacon on it and even adds two blueberry muffins.

I walk behind Jane and kiss her cheek, giving her shoulder a gentle squeeze. Jules is nowhere in sight. It takes everything inside of me not to ask where she is.

"Morning, Jane."

She grabs my hand resting on her shoulder, giving it a gentle squeeze, and lets out a harsh exhale. "Good to have you here, Jessie. That sweet little girl hasn't quit worrying if you'd show up."

I gaze over at Whit, who has her tongue poking out of the corner of her lips while she concentrates on pouring a glass of orange juice. A Waylon Jennings song blares from upstairs. Jane fidgets with her notebook, all the while holding back the impending tears. I keep my hand on her shoulder until my sweet girl brings over my plate of food. She rushes back to the counter to grab the glass of orange juice. It sloshes over the sides, but her smile never breaks.

My girl. Insane how natural that flows from my thoughts. Never have I felt such intense love for a person.

"Jessie, bacon time." Whit grins up at me, tugging on my hand.

I take the seat next to Jane, moving my hand from her shoulder to clutch her hand on the table. Whit chatters on about not being able to wear a neon tutu. Jane chuckles every once in a while.

Whit shoots a finger out at Jane. "You know Papa loved my tutus. He bought me all of them. He'd even let me fall asleep in them. This is crap I can't wear one the day he goes to see the angels."

Jane shakes her head; tears spill over her rounded cheeks. They're happy ones. Ones made of memories. "You're right, baby girl. Papa never told you no once."

"See." Whit plants her hands on her hips, chucking up her chin. "I'm wearing it. I hid it deep in the closet so Momma couldn't go crazy on it."

Shit. Okay, this is where I should be stepping in saying something all wisdomey. The reality is I have no goddamn right. I threw that away years ago when I was an arrogant, self-centered asshole.

"Baby girl, you know Nana never tells you no either, but today is a tough day for—"

Jane's words are cut off when a loud crash from upstairs echoes through the house. I'm up and moving before anyone can stop me. I hear Jane distract Whit as I race up the stairs. The clatter doesn't cease. It does the opposite and intensifies. The high decibel of glass shattering and ricocheting off walls greets me as I swing open the door to Jules' bedroom.

The depressing country song fades into "Jack & Diane" by John Mellencamp. I have no idea what

I've just walked into. My Jules is crumpled in the middle of the floor along with the shards of glass. A picture frame lies feet away from her, and then I see the photo of the two of us crumpled against her closet.

None of that phases me. I couldn't care less if the love of my life just threw me out the window. No, it's her crushed stature that halts me and breaks my heart all in the same moment. It's as if the years of stress, heartache, and joy have taken their toll and she's calling it quits.

Her pale pink fingernails clutch to a shiny black leather strap around her ankle where she's inches away from buckling it. Her tanned, toned legs peek out from underneath a sleek black dress that shakes as her cries take over.

"Jules." I take a step towards her.

She doesn't hear me. Jules is wrapped up in her storm of torment and torture. The violent circles of clouds and rain pummel her, not giving any sign of relenting. She's held it all together for everyone. The invisible dam gave out. The bricks are crumbling to the ground.

I call her name one more time, getting no response. It's too much for my tender and regretful heart to take. Old habits take over. I stride to her, scoop her up in my arms, and settle on the edge of her bed to avoid any shards of glass.

"Jules, baby, you're okay."

Still, she doesn't respond. Her entire body rattles against my chest. The wetness of her sadness soaks into my white dress shirt. Jules doesn't tense up or battle back. Instead, she curls up into my chest.

Her body is exhausted from the past days, and I'm no fool, knowing she's worn down from the last several years. Her soul can't take another beating because there's nothing to back her up.

"Shhhh, baby, shhhh. I got you." I rock back and forth, keeping her cradled to my chest. "Let it out, Jules, I got you."

"I hate you."

I barely make out her muffled cries. The words pierce my heart with a damn sharp, heated dagger. I deserve every single shard of her hatred.

"I hate you." She balls up her fists, pounding into my chest. "I hate you because I fucking still love you and you told me to take care of it. I did. My papa is dead. My world is once again crumbling around my feet, and I can't do a damn thing."

Jules rambles on, beating out all of our past, letting it land square on my chest. She holds nothing back. I can't speak a single word because every syllable that escapes her lips is God's honest truth.

All I can do is rock her back and forth. It's my due punishment for my past sins. A Chris Stapleton song begins to stream throughout the bedroom, and the soothing melody calms Jules' angry cries into pure sorrow.

"She loved him. Papa was Whit's greatest joy every month he visited. They were peas in a pod. She hasn't fully realized what has happened. Then we threw out the whole 'dad' card. She's going to crash and tumble like I have since graduation. And how is my nana going to go on? It's too much, Jessie. God, make it stop." She balls her fists around my collar, tugging me closer to her.

I don't hesitate, giving in to her. I shelter her with my whole being and will continue to do so. It's the reason I was put on this earth. I fucked up, and that's no secret. But the thing is I'll continue to fix that fuck up until my dying day. I remain silent, letting Jules get everything out.

One hand clutches her ass while the other one roams up her back while I continue rocking back and forth. Several more songs flow by until I realize Jules' sobs have slowed. Her still frame lies limp in my arms. I reach down and buckle her damn high heel, the demon that catapulted Jules into her turmoil. I'm no damn fool, knowing it was the final straw that broke her. I can only thank God I'm the one to hold her as she captures herself once again.

I've spent endless nights knowing precisely what it meant for her to come back to this small, one-horse town. It wasn't an easy task for her. Hell, I know above anyone else all the demons she's beat to get here.

My palms warm against her flesh. I grip her ass to me, relishing the feel. Old memories attack, and I want nothing more to have her back in my life. I'll never stop until it happens.

Her sobs quiet and body goes still. I brush a hand through her long, loose curls and kiss the top of her head.

"You're going to get through this, baby. Jules, you are one of the strongest women I know. Your papa was always so damn proud of you and would want you there today holding Nana and Whit's hands. I'm going to be right by your side."

She doesn't say a word. I take it as a good sign

and stand up. I walk carefully over to her bathroom. Beams of sunlight shine through the open window, giving off the perfect glow. I grimace once I set her ass on the counter; the loss of contact kills me. Jules doesn't let go, keeping her arms laced around my neck.

"Let's get this cleaned up and make your papa proud." I swipe along the mascara cascading below both of her gorgeous eyes. The light makeup she was wearing smears down her face in sorrow and grief.

Jules doesn't move, acknowledging my touch. It's everything and nothing at all. I get these few raw and honest moments with her when she lets down her shield.

"Jessie."

"Yeah, baby." I run my hand up into her hair. My palm sizzles against the flesh of her cheeks.

"Take it all away. You were the only person that ever could."

Fuck, I know more than anyone else I don't deserve this. But like a dry desert that needs water, I lean forward. Her lips are the water I crave. Once our lips connect, it's powerful and dangerous. It's like the old times. The chemistry entangles us into a damn tangled thorned-up bush that you fall deeper and deeper into the more you struggle to get free.

Her skin tastes the same from years ago. It's perfection and sweetness at its honesty. Jules leans forward, dipping her tongue into my mouth. My knees buckle, yet I don't pull away. I enjoy and devour every lap and the taste of my girl. Her torso melts into mine. Her fists balled into my collar tug me down closer to her.

A door slams from downstairs, snapping us from our lust-bound trance. I don't miss the wince vibrating from Jules as if she's recognized her mistake. I ignore it, dropping my forehead to hers. Her eyes snap shut, and the pain and hurt lace every single one of her features. This isn't going to be easy, but I know one thing for damn sure—I'm not giving up this time. I'll chase this woman across the country.

"Jules, don't."

She doesn't respond.

"Don't close up on me, please. We have to handle this."

"Jessie, there's nothing to handle." Her knuckles grow white, still clutching to my shirt.

"You know that's a damn lie, and that kiss just proved it."

"Jessie—"

"Listen to me, please." I gently raise her face to mine and wait until she shoots those beautiful cornflower blue eyes my direction. "Friends. We can be friends. We have so much to work through. I ask you please don't shut me out."

Beats of silence vibrate between us. An eternity passes before Jules parts those perfect plump lips.

"I can do that," she whispers.

"Yeah?" I jerk my chin, keeping her chin tilted up to me.

She nods while a slight pink blush covers her cheeks.

Her eyes flutter shut. "Yes, Jessie. As much as I hate admitting it, I need you back in my life."

"I fucking promise, Jules. I'm here and not leaving or pushing you away, nor will I accept you pushing me away. I don't deserve you, but goddammit, I'm going to fight like hell for you. If friendship is all you can give me, I'll accept it like a hungry beggar on the corner."

She nods once again. It's not the answer I was hoping for but better than an ass chewing. She's exhausted and defeated. Today can't get over fast enough. Once the service and dinner is over, I'm hauling her ass right back here and letting her sleep while I hang out with Whit.

I do my best to wipe away the streaks of black from her face, dotting a tissue under her eyes.

"You look gorgeous." I lean down and kiss her forehead. "Let's go," I whisper into her temple, allowing my lips to stay put for several seconds as I lace our fingers together.

Jules hops off the counter, tightening her hand in mine. I lead her out of her room and down the stairs. A mess of a black dress fluttering around the bottom steps comes into view. Whit's twirling and hopping from toe to toe to the beat of an old Elvis song.

The creaking of the old stairs gains her attention. She freezes mid-move, all her attention focused solely on Jules and me. Her gaze goes between our faces then down to our linked hands. The slice of time freezes for what feels like an eternity.

Jane walks up behind Whit with her game face on for the funeral. Only those who know her well would pick up on the fact she's seconds away from crumbling just like her daughter did.

Whit claps her hands together, bringing my attention back to her. Her eyes light up, and every single tiny tooth in her mouth dazzles.

"Momma and Daddy!" she squeals in a high-pitched voice.

We don't have a chance to react before she bounces up the bottom two steps and collides into our legs. Jules and I stare at each other, both at a loss for words.

"Thank you," I whisper. The only two words that are worthy of speaking.

A genuine smile plays across Jules' lips. Whirlwind Whit manages to break between the two of us, grabbing each of our hands until she's the one holding us, the link bonding us together forever. The one that will never be shattered. My ugly past and poor choices threaten to taint the moment. I don't let them. I could beat myself up for the rest of my life and not enjoy the tomorrows. It's impossible to fall in that cycle with my sweet little girl beaming up at me.

"Daddy, you look sexy," Whit says, finishing with a giggle.

Jules gasps, and Jane stifles her giggles.

I clear my throat and swing our linked hands. "Well, thank you."

"Nana said so, and she also said you're working damn hard to get back in Momma's—"

"Whit!" Jane exclaims. "We need to put the chickens up before we go."

I shake my head. This might be the first time I've ever seen Jane flushed with embarrassment. Whit bounds over to her, and she ushers her right out the door. As soon as the screen door slams shut, my spine stiffens. This is all happening way too fast and just when I talked Jules off a cliff. I have no idea how she'll respond to the comment. Thing is, Jane hit the nail on the head. I'm fighting for my girl.

Jules takes three steps back from me. Her expression is unreadable.

"Baby, friends, remember."

She shakes her head, causing her brown curls to tumble and toss over her shoulders.

Chapter 10

Jules

It's all too much—this crazy, insane rollercoaster ride that never ends, sending my guts and brain sailing in different directions. It's enough, and I burst wide open. It's not tears this time. No, it's the complete opposite. Seeing my little Whit about to say Jessie was trying too damn hard to get in my pants was the final hit to the tender thread of sanity holding me together.

I throw my head back with the first bark of deep laughter escaping me. Soon tears stream down my face, my belly begins to cramp in giggle pains, and it doesn't stop for long moments. Jessie's hands land on top of my shoulders. When I glance up to the concerned look on his face, I fall even deeper into my crazed outburst.

He pulls me to his chest. His vibrations of laughter ricochet into my skin and soul. God, I need to push this man away. I should for my sanity and the sole purpose of surviving. The harsh truth is I can't because he'll always be a part of my life. I can't block him out because of Whit. Reality brought me here, and it's something I can never escape. I can only pray for my heart.

"You better now?" Jessie mumbles down into the top of my head.

The laughter has subsided, and I have no other option than to melt into his body. I nod against his chest, my arms wrapping around his middle and holding on for security. I may hate the man or, hell, have hated him, but right now he's my security and temple of stability.

Jessie silently steps back, grabs my hand, and leads me out the front door. He never lets go of my hand, not even on the ride to the cemetery, not even when Whit insists on sitting on his lap in the backseat of the funeral home's limo. I didn't even have the energy to require she be buckled in. The short half-mile drive didn't last long. Jessie's hand never leaves mine as we exit the car.

For that, I am thankful since all the prying stares are aimed directly at my little girl and me. Whit squeezes my other hand, and with the two of them, I hold my head high, following Nana to the front row. All the faces blur into one dark cloud. Whit's constant fidgeting keeps me grounded just enough to avoid another complete freak-out.

She sits on Jessie's lap right next to me, flipping the hem of my black dress up and down. Any other day, I'd lose my shit on her, but not today. It is soothing and the perfect sense of calm I need.

Nana is a perfect picture of bravery. Her shoulders never quake throughout the ceremony nor does she flinch when the gunshots fire off into the sky in honor of Papa's military service. Between her stoic behavior and Whit wiggling next to me, I'm able to keep it all together. We shake hands and share hugs with all the people who came out today. I couldn't tell you who I saw or didn't see. I didn't miss the sideways glances Jessie sent nosy folks, warning them to stay clear of me today.

Then I see her. Her face is the only one that's vibrant and clear as day—Shayna. She glides right up to Nana, insincere and as fake as the day she was born. I try my best not to look at her dazzling designer high heels and skimpy-ass dress. I'm sure it came from some famous and overpriced designer. I smooth my palms down the black dress from Walmart and do my best to ignore all of my former insecurities. They have the power to chop me down right in front of everyone. Jessie being Whit's dad would be yesterday's news in this small town. The coffee talk at Gravy Dave's would be quite the event.

"I'm so sorry for your loss," she coos, wrapping her arms around Nana.

She offers me a sideways glance, but my body language does nothing to offer my openness. It only lasts for a few seconds since her stare goes right to Jessie. I can't miss what she wanted or thought she had. He was clear as day about all of it. Still doesn't make it an easy pill to swallow. She had loved him, or thought she had. Cody stopped by the other day, filling me in on all of it. Damn little town gossip knew it all. Shayna wanted the prestige of being on his arm, and that's where their story ended. Doesn't make it any better knowing Jessie was in a relationship with her and possibly damn close to proposing. He chose to settle, and that's just another shard of glass to my torn and battered heart.

"Daddy!" Whit tugs on Jessie's dress shirt while bouncing up and down. "Daddy!"

Jessie doesn't give two shits Shayna is standing before him. He glances down, giving our daughter his complete attention. When his muscular back and broad shoulders bend down to get on her level, something inside of me tears open raw wounds. It's a picture I've wanted to see for years.

Whit does her best to whisper even though it comes out as a shout. "I have to pee, like now."

Jessie whips his head up to me with a hundred questions plastered across his face. It may not be appropriate, but a playful smirk covers my face. Even through the deep canals of sorrow, the image before me is too damn adorable. I give him a nod of my head. It jerks him into action as he stands to his feet and ushers her away.

Shayna's stomping and huffing brings me back to the present. I've always heard about steam billowing out of someone's ears, and Jesus, I can see it right before my eyes. Shayna has swarms of hornets flowing out of her ears. Even her couture makeup can't cover her anger. I give her a nod and go to the next guest greeting Nana. The process repeats itself. When I realize Jessie and Whit haven't returned in a few minutes, I escape the greeting line. A part of me feels like shit while the other half doesn't. Because it's what being a mom is.

It doesn't take me long to track Whit's squeals and Jessie's barks. I round the last row of headstones and waltz behind the line of fir trees to see Whit, who has her dress up around her chest and Jessie covering his eyes.

"Dad, I can't pee on my dress. Are you serious there's no bathroom out here?"

"Baby girl, there's no bathroom. You have to pee on the ground." Jessie shrugs in his dress shirt, keeping his eyes masked.

"Dad, I might pee on my dress." Whit lowers her head, trying to figure out how this is all going to work. Growing up in the city hasn't gifted her with many opportunities to pee outside.

I shrink behind the lush branches of the fir tree, enjoying the scene before me. Jessie tilts his face to the heavens with his hand still covering his eyes.

"Daddy, I'm about to have an accident. I've never had one." Whit's voice trembles and shakes. A true sign of impending tears to come.

Jessie picks up on it too, jumping into action. His hand drops from his eyes, and he's at her side. It takes all of my God-given willpower to remain in place.

"I'm going to hold your dress, okay, baby? You just squat and do your business. I'll be looking at the clouds." Jessie curls the fluff of Whit's black dress and looks back to the heavens.

All of the worries of the world float away watching the scene before me. It's a picture-perfect scenario, not one even the most talented artist could swipe across a canvas. This is life. The hatred I've kept harbored down in my belly doesn't matter;

none of that poison matters watching the two of them. It's picture perfect.

"I didn't pee on my dress." Whit bounces up, nearly knocking Jessie in the bridge of his nose. He's faster than her. I don't miss the fact he grimaces and grabs for his injured knee.

"I did it, Daddy." Whit continues to clap.

Jessie doesn't celebrate until her little dress is put back in place entirely. Once all the tender material tumbles into place, he holds out his arms. Whit doesn't think twice before bounding into his chest. It's my final undoing. My knees go weak, and my heart hammers against my sternum. It's all surreal and life changing. Some things you can never process—like the scene that lies before me.

"Whit, we have a fan." Jess's gruff and timber voice echoes across the trees, and before I know it, he's rounding the brush with Whit in his arms.

"Mom, that was wild." Whit brushes her bangs from her face. "I did it. Only little bits of pees went up on my calves."

I cringe internally, knowing all too well what it's like to pee outside and the inevitable splashes that splat on your legs. Whit's toothy smile is contagious. I find myself mirroring hers. Once Jessie is right next to me, I lean in and kiss Whit's cheek then glance up to the heavens.

Whit's Papa would be smiling from ear to ear. He loved the country life. It bled in his heart and soul. He wanted nothing more than for me to take over the farm. I'll never forget the grumbling coming from him about Whit being raised in a city.

"This damn townhouse and taxis are no place for

a damn young soul to thrive. Come home, Jules."

Hearing his words tickle my ears doesn't bring tears to my eyes but a smile gracing my lips. It's perfection. Even though he's gone and the whole town will soon be analyzing my life choices and daughter with a magnifying glass, none of it bothers me a bit. The only thing that matters is the scene before me. I've been reborn in the worst of circumstances.

"Papa would be so proud," I whisper in her ear.

Whit's smile shines broader at the same time Jessie laces his hand in mine. He doesn't have to say a word before he leads us back to the crowd of people. My two rocks stand beside me while the rest of our family friends say their piece. Whit leaps and jumps in Jessie's lap on the ride back to the ranch.

She plays up the theme of being in the limo by fluttering in Jessie's lap and pretending to sip out of a plastic champagne glass. I don't even have any damn idea why we are in a limo. It's the perfect distraction for all of us. Even Nana clutches her belly as laughter attacks her.

The barn is full of familiar faces. The old equipment has been moved out, and the space is now lined with tables, chairs, and food.

"How?" The one word escapes my lips

Jessie clutches my hand. "Knew your papa would want all of his family and friends celebrating here."

"You did this?" It comes out as a question even though it's an answer. "When?"

"Doesn't matter. He deserves it." Jessie kisses Whit's cheek while guiding us into the barn.

It's a swarm of chaos with familiar faces, all sincere and caring. I'm no fool and damn well know there are curious stares and judging eyes.

"Daddy, I'm hungry." Whit points to the long line of food.

The poor girl has no idea that some of those casseroles look amazing and taste like shit. Jessie doesn't miss a beat, striding right over to the long tables of food. He places her down on her feet, grabbing a plate for her and himself. He tucks the napkins and plastic silverware in his back pocket. Whit points at the green salad, making me internally grin. Then she's off to the cheese-soaked casseroles. Jessie does his best scooping up food for himself as she continues down the table.

Old Man Jenkin, who owns the local hardware store, stops Jessie. It's clear Jenkin is well into the conversation while Jessie keeps an eye on Whit, doing his best to keep up with the conversation.

I ignore all the chatter surrounding me and only nod when I hear certain words. Whit has all of my attention with Jessie in second place. The guy has been thrust into fatherhood, and by damn, like anything else, he's a natural.

"Is that girl normal?" Jenkin's voice floats across the barn.

I follow his line of sight to see that Whit has managed to dip her fingertips in black olives. She's waggling them in front of her face, popping one in her mouth and then dipping her finger right back in the bowl to snag more. She tosses a few raw onion rings on her plate along with slivered dill pickles. Yeah, those are the only things she'll be devouring and sneaking back up to the table for more. I buy onions and dill pickles in stock back at home.

Home. The thought shatters me. I am home. I'm thinking about California. My phone dings in my clutch, and I pull it out. It's my publisher, reminding me of the tight deadline I'm on for my second round of edits. It's not an option but rather a do-or-die type scenario.

Jessie's shoulders tighten and bristle up at Old Man Jenkin. "She's just fine. Worry about your own damn business."

And with that, Jessie rushes behind Whit, who bounds to a lonely table. She's managed to eat five more olives off of her fingers. Tears spill down my cheeks without warning when she dips her dainty fingers on Jessie's plate, stealing his heap of olives. "Go to them," Nana whispers in my ear.

I flick my gaze over to her, wiping away the unwanted and stray tears with the back of my hand.

"That's your future. Go, baby girl." She urges me on by pushing my hips forward.

I never had a chance of falling out of love with Jessie. So I nod my head and walk right over to my future. I have no idea what that future looks like. I do know Jessie will be a part of it—one way or another.

"Want me to make you a plate, Jules?" Jessie reaches for my hand the moment I'm at the table.

I shake my head. "Not hungry right now."

Jessie pushes his plate to me when I take the seat on the other side of Whit. "Wasn't much of Mom's sausage casserole left. Grabbed as much as I could. You used to love it."

"It's yummy, Momma." Whit scoops a mouthful of the creamy potato sausage mixture in her mouth. Her smile is damn contagious. I can't help myself from finishing off Jessie's part of the potatoes.

Chapter 11

Jessie

My spine stiffens when my parents take the seats across from us. I told them about Whit, and to say my mom was crushed and my dad was devastated would be a significant understatement of vast proportions.

The glistening tears brimming in my mom's wise eyes let me know she's doing her best to keep her emotions contained. She wants more than anything to scoop Whit up in her arms and shower her in love. I told her today wasn't the day, and hell, even tomorrow might not be. Whit has enough stuff to process and work through, as does Jules. I'm damn shocked and amazed how well Whit has handled everything so far. She's a damn tough girl.

"Hi, Carolyn and Tim." Jules wipes around her mouth with a napkin, offering them both a warm smile.

She used to be like a second daughter to them. I don't allow myself to creep down that lane of self-loathing and being pissed off at myself. I ruined so damn much but now have an opportunity to right all of my wrongs.

"Who are you guys?" Whit points her finger with an olive on the end of it at my parents.

Their eyes grow wide and jaws slack a tick. I lean in on the table and catch Whit's attention then brush back a lock of her hair.

"Those are my parents." I keep eye contact, wanting to see her response.

She nods and nibbles on the olive. "Makes sense because you look like your dad, but he's way older."

She drags out the word out, causing all of us to erupt in laughter. And just like that, Whit healed the situation, not even knowing she was doing it. I lean down and kiss the top of her head.

"Love you, little girl."

She nods, focusing on her olives. Mom and Whit fall into easy conversation, even venturing around the barn. Dad has long escaped into conversation about farming and cattle. Jules stays slumped in her seat, not saying a word, taking in the scene in front of her. She never takes her attention off Jane for very long. She didn't even flinch when I scooted into the chair next to her and laced my fingers with hers.

Our peaceful bliss is interrupted when a high, shrill, piercing cry enters the barn. Jules is up on her feet and racing to the entrance. Most of the people have been long gone; only close family friends linger about. I race past a line of women covering casserole dishes.

Jules' hair flows behind her as she races over to Whit, who's on the ground still wailing. My mom is on her knees at her side. The old tire swing blows around next to the scene.

Jules pulls Whit into her, kissing the top of her head and running a hand up and down her back.

"Daddy!" Whit manages to get out between her sobs. She holds her hands up to me.

I bend down and grab her without a second thought. She tucks her wet face in the crook of my neck and wraps her arms around my neck.

"What happened?" I ask, running circles on her back like Jules was doing seconds ago.

"She wanted to stand on top of the swing and show me a dance move. I told her it was too dangerous, and when I turned my back…" Mom's tears dance in her own eyes.

Jules places a hand on Mom's forearm. "It's fine, Carolyn. That's Whit for you. If her mind was set on it, she wouldn't stop until she tried it out."

"I don't think anything is broken. She just knocked the wind out of herself," Mom replies. "I checked everything."

That eases the worry right out of me. Mom was a nurse for years before retiring. Whit's sobs continue.

Jules steps up to us, reaching up on her tiptoes to whisper in her ear. "You're okay, baby girl. You need to relax and next time listen when an adult tells you something."

Whit's chest wracks against mine as she does her best to calm herself down.

"I'll take her upstairs and take a nap with her," I

offer. "That way you can stay down here and see if your nana needs anything."

Jules nibbles on her bottom lip, nervous about the whole idea. I don't push her and give her time to think it through.

"Please, Momma," Whit mumbles in my chest.

"Yeah, I'll be up in a bit. A nap does sound pretty damn good right now." Jules kisses Whit's cheek then grabs my mom's hand. I watch the two of them disappear through the opening of the old barn.

By the time I make it up the staircase, Whit's breathing has evened out. She doesn't even budge when I lay her in the bed. I glance out Jules' childhood bedroom window with the barn coming into view. I'm torn between going out there and helping or lying down next to my sweet girl.

Whit's light snores win over my heart. I toe off my boots and undo the first few buttons of my dress shirt before settling in next to her.

"Daddy," she mumbles and rolls over to face me while snuggling down in my chest.

"I'm here." I brush away the hair matted to her face from her tears.

"You promise you're not going to get too busy again?"

I can barely make out the words between the sleep attacking them. I tug her to my chest, holding her as close as possible.

"Baby, I promise. Don't you ever worry about that."

My eyelids grow heavy with Whit's rhythmic breathing lulling me to sleep. Her sweet scent of lingering cherries is the last thing I remember before giving in to sleep.

***

Jules

"I never thought they'd get the hell out of here." Nana plops down in Papa's recliner.

"Me too." I kick back my foot and unstrap each shoe. "I'm going to go check on Whit then be right back."

"Good, because I need a drinking partner tonight." Nana flashes a smile at me.

My black heels dangle off my fingertips. I shake my head. Nana is quite the light drinker, but I have a feeling she's really going to tie one on.

The stairs creak as I tiptoe up them. The sound is deafening in the quiet house. I peek through the open door to my room before entering.

A genuine smile graces my lips as I lean on the doorjamb, watching Jessie's hulking frame with Whit curled up in his side. It's picture perfect and oh so effortless. I find myself easing next to the bed, leaning over and kissing Whit's forehead, then my lips glide across the scruff of Jessie's jaw. The sensation coursing through me makes me drunk while my heart squeezes painfully. It was natural and not even an action I had to think twice about.

Reaching behind me, I go to unzip my dress. I'm startled when a large palm glides up my back and undoes it for me. I clutch the material to my chest and peer over my shoulder. Jessie stares up at me through sleepy eyes. I press my finger to my lips, and he nods.

I pad into the bathroom and slip out of my dress, climbing into a well-loved pair of yoga pants and a baggy shirt. Jessie is out when I grab my MacBook and slip out of the room. I reach behind me and run my hand over the place his palm grazed down my skin. My flesh sears to life.

"They out?" Nana asks as I take the last step.

She's armed with one of Papa's bottles of bourbon, two tumblers, and ice.

"They are. Exhaustion finally won over with my little girl."

"You were just like her when you were little. You'd go and go and go until you couldn't anymore. It typically ended with you in tears and Jessie crashing next to you on the couch." She pours a stout glass of bourbon.

"Do you think I'm a fool for letting him back in so easily?" I ask, curling my legs on the couch and setting my MacBook in my lap.

"I think you'd be a fool not to give it another chance. You never know what tomorrow will bring. I'd say love the hell out of anyone you want and live with no regrets." She takes her first gulp of the drink and then passes me mine.

I humor her by taking light sips. There's no way in hell I want another hangover like the last one, but there's something so peaceful and serene about sharing this moment with her. A sweet ending to one of the hardest days of our lives.

She makes damn good on her promise, pounding the bourbon and telling her favorite stories about

Papa. I listen to each word while accepting changes in my manuscript and polishing up a few spots that needed desperate attention.

A massive smile forms on my face when I press the send button on the email. Finishing a book never grows old. It's happiness and accomplishment all balled together, then the nerves settle in. It's like sending your first born to preschool and not being able to stand by their side to protect them.

Nana's light snores float around in the living room. She drifted off a few minutes ago. I grab Papa's blanket and wrap her up in it. I'm shocked I haven't heard any movement upstairs. That means Whit will be up super early in the morning since she's still out. I creep up the stairs and pause halfway, glancing back down at the living room and back up to my room. I nibble on my bottom lip, trying to decide what to do. My body has one idea it's certain about, and my mind screams another thing.

"Live your life, Jules. Do what makes you happy."

It's as if I can hear my papa's voice encouraging me to be me and live life. It's something he had to do when my world was turned upside down. No more what-ifs. It's time to follow my heart. It's always belonged to one man.

Whit has wiggled to the side of the bed with Jessie sprawled out in the center, leaving me just enough room to cuddle up to his other side. I slip my hands underneath the soft cotton t-shirt and slip my bra off. I toss my reading glasses on the nightstand. Getting older and spending more time on the computer hasn't been easy on the eyes. I just haven't bitten the bullet and bought prescription glasses yet.

The bed dips as my knee sinks into its softness. I ease my way in the bed, tugging a bit on the pillow just enough to rest my head on. Jessie stirs a bit. I notice he still has his socks on. I creep down and tug them off then pull a blanket up to cover all three of us. Jessie stretches out on his back. I have no idea if he's awake or dead asleep. He gives nothing away. His silent offer of shelter stretches out next to me.

I curl up into his side, splaying my hand over his chest. I let it linger there for several seconds before reaching over to rest my hand on Whit's back. I snuggle down deeper, inhaling the scent of my home.

Jessie's free arm falls by my side. He palms my ass, pulling me closer to home. I have no worries in the world when my eyes flutter shut, and that's something I haven't said in years.

Chapter 12

Jessie

"See ya, Coach." Monty, a rookie, waves as he jogs off the field. It's been a week since I woke up with both of my girls snuggled in at my side. It hasn't happened again, and that fact guts me every night when I lie down on my cold, frigid sheets. Not much sleep ever comes as I toss and turn, knowing what's missing from my life.

Jules has pulled back from me. There's been no hand holding or shared tender kisses. She talks minimally at most to me. The one thing she hasn't done is keep Whit from me. As promised, I get to take her to dance class. Today is her second class, and I may be more excited than her.

"Jessie."

I glance down to Whit, who's keeping up at my side. I smile at the cuteness and don't even care that she calls me by my name now and then. I was shocked as hell when Jules let her come to practice with me. Whit got wind of it and begged her mom.

Works out perfectly since her dance class is in fifteen minutes. If I would've had to run out to the farm and back into town, we for sure would've been a good ten minutes late.

"What, baby girl?" I adjust the bag of the footballs slung over my shoulder.

"Why did you tell that nice boy he'd better run like a motherfucker like his ass was on fire?"

I clear my throat, nearly choking on my own tongue. My spine stiffens, and it takes everything inside of me not to freeze in my steps.

"What did you say?" I clutch the strings of the football bag until my knuckles grow white. "Wait. Never mind, don't answer that. You were wearing headphones practicing a new dance on the bleachers. How did you hear me?"

She ducks her head, glancing at the ground. "Your face turned really red like you were trying to poop. One time Momma couldn't poop, and her tummy hurt. Her face looked like yours. I got worried, so I took off my headphones and heard you yelling, 'Run, motherfucker, like your ass is on fire.'"

I drop to one knee, placing a gentle hand on the top of her shoulder. "Whit, never repeat those words."

"Which ones?" She tilts her head in question.

"The very bad ones. I'm pretty sure you know what I'm talking about."

"Motherfucker and ass?" She bites her bottom lip, trapping a smile, but I can sense a storm brewing behind her loving eyes.

Oh, this girl can play her cards damn well.

"Yes, those words." I take a deep breath, drop the ball bag, and grip the top of my ball cap that's placed backward on my head. "They're adult words and ugly ones at that. I get pretty fired up when I'm coaching. I'll try better when you're around, okay?"

She nods. Her eyes well up with tears, but none spill over. Her mischievous smile is long gone in the hot summer breeze. "Momma hates football. She doesn't hate anything but football. I've seen her cry over it."

"Whit." Her name ghosts off my lips. "Baby, it's okay."

I cradle the back of her head and bring it to my chest, running my palm up and down her back.

She sobs into my neck. "You love football. It's your favorite like dance is mine. And Momma hates it. You're going to get too busy with football, aren't you, Jessie?"

Her words make me flop back down to my ass. I bring her with me, keeping my sweet baby girl clutched to my chest, soaking up all of her innocent worries. Not one day will go by that I don't regret my decision to be a selfish prick. I've damaged far more things than I ever thought. It's going to take years to prove to my little girl that I won't be going anywhere or, for that fact, miss spending a day with her.

I open my mouth to reassure her, but the words clog deep in my throat. The honest truth is there are no words that can fix or even begin to heal the wound I've inflicted on this sweet soul. It's going to take repeated action in Whit's life until there's no doubt or worry left in her mind.

"I hear you, baby." I kiss the top of her head. "I do love football. It is my dance. But it will never ever come between me and you or your mom, for that fact. I promise, baby girl. I know this is scary and so new for you. I promise you that I'll show you every single day that I'll never be too busy for you."

Again. Again, I think in my head that was the biggest mistake of my life. I could beat myself up for it while drowning in a bottle of whiskey, but there's this little girl in my lap who means so much more.

I give Whit time to dry her tears and pull herself together. I reach down, fluffing out her neon tutu when she peers up at me. Her tears have vanished, and that contagious toothy grin reappears.

"I know, Daddy. It's just scary. Momma has been crying every night, and so has Nana. I'm just nervous."

"That's okay, honey." I cup her face. "It's all natural. We are all feeling crazy and different emotions. It's good that you can talk about them and not keep them bottled up. You know you can always talk to me about anything, right?"

She nods her head then peers down at the sparkles on the front of her t-shirt. She begins twirling one of them around.

"And Whit, if you don't like coming to football practice with me, you don't have to. I want you to be happy."

Her crazy curls whip up in my direction. "Daddy, I love it. Makes me feel kinda bad because Momma hates it. But up in those stands, it felt like the biggest stage for me to practice on."

I glance over to the aluminum bleachers. They're nothing fancy and average in size, but I can see how they'd look in her eyes. In the middle of them, there's a large platform where the school band sets up and plays during home games. I'm taken back to memories of Jules and me making out underneath them so many years ago. Hell, we even went further than that.

I glance back at her and tap her nose. "Then anytime you want to come, you can."

She hops up from my lap, spinning in a circle and shaking her little hips, then holds out a hand to me. "I'll help you, Daddy."

She has no idea how much power are in those four simple words. It's the key with the potential to unlock a world of answers I've been chasing for the last five years. I reach up and hold onto her petite hand. I pretend it's Whit who pulls me up with all her strength.

After grabbing the ball bag, I grab her hand, and we begin walking to my truck. I toss the bag in the bed of the truck and then hoist Whit up into the passenger seat. I bought a booster seat just for my truck, and it happened to be pink and sparkly with little ballerinas fluttering all over it.

"Daddy." She grabs my hand once I click the buckle.

"Yeah." I look down at her, wondering what is coming next.

"Momma says 'you rotten bastards' all the time while driving in California." She covers her mouth with her free hand and giggles behind it.

"Oh, Whit." I ruffle her hair and do my best not to laugh at her adorable innocence and zest for life. She's a breath of fresh air in a world filled with stress and longing. I give in, unable to hold it in any longer. I throw my head back to the heavens and roar out my laughter. The harder I laugh, the louder Whit's giggles grow. It continues for extended minutes. It's the perfect release from the intense conversation on the football field.

***

My skin crawls as the prying eyes of women I went to high school with rake up and down my body along with the other women in town. The judgmental stares commenced the day after Jules' grandfather was buried. The town whispers are loud enough to deafen a person. In the true fashion of gossip, not one brave soul has dared to approach me about it.

I don't give these nosey no-goods a second glance. My vision stays focused on my little girl who outshines everyone in her class. While the other girls struggle to keep up with the instructions, Whit is a step ahead of her teacher. She practices a new move and has it down.

This session she's enrolled in a hip-hop class. Didn't stop her from wearing her tutu and pirouetting every chance she could get. She'd stripped off her sparkly shirt once her foot stepped into the dance studio only to reveal a bedazzled leotard or whatever in the hell they're called.

When class is called, Whit doesn't rush to me

like the other girls do their parents. She faces the wall covered in mirrors, drops her head for a few beats, and then flawlessly goes through the new dance she was taught today, not missing a beat. She does all of this without one single note of music.

Goddamn pride like no other swells in my chest. This isn't some silly infatuation of a little girl. It's her passion. I can see it in her eyes, the determination on each of her features, the sheer concentration she puts into every move, and above all the dazzling smile when she finishes.

I stand to my feet once she executes the last move and begin slowly clapping. Whit whips her head in my direction with a heart-stopping grin that I'll never forget. It's the promise of a future I don't deserve but am damn willing to take and make the best of it.

"Did you like it, Daddy?" Whit races over to me.

I bend down just in time to scoop her up in my arms. Hers go tight around my neck. I probably squeeze a bit too tight but can't help it.

"I loved it, baby girl. Holy crap, you're amazing."

Yeah, not the best choice of words. But it does explain exactly how I feel. I don't miss the hushed whispers about wondering how Shayna was doing with all of this. I'd be a liar if I said it didn't make my blood boil. I ignore them because of the sweetest gift in my arms overpowers and trumps everything.

Once Whit's feet hit the ground, she races off to her dance instructor, who's talking to another woman. She waits patiently until she's finished.

"Do you need something, Whit?" The instructor turns to her, bending down to get on her level.

Whit shakes her head. "No, I just wanted to tell you thank you for class."

Will this girl ever cease to amaze me?

"You are so welcome, sweetie." The young teacher wraps her up in a hug. "I love having you in class."

Whit beams with pride and then races back over to me. She tucks her shoes back in her bag that has her name embroidered on it while slipping on her flip-flops. I know none of this shit is cheap. It amazes me how Jules pulled all of this off over the years.

"Ready?" I hold my hand out.

Whit grimaces and then dances around. "I have to potty, Daddy."

"Okay." We scope out the bathroom, and I usher her over to it.

She's not in the bathroom for thirty seconds before she's calling out for help. I drop my head to the door and grumble to myself. I can handle anything with her, but this has to be the most awkward shit ever.

"Daddy!" she squeals.

I take a deep breath and twist the doorknob. This time I force myself not to cover my eyes, knowing it only makes the situation that much more awkward for everyone involved. She has the leotard thingy all twisted up around her torso while she continues to dance in place. Her eyes widen, and rosy cheeks let me know she's seconds away from having an accident.

I leap into action, no longer worrying about being uncomfortable. I get everything untwisted and slid down her body. Whit doesn't waste a second before leaping up onto the toilet.

"Okay, Daddy, turn around and cover your eyes," she chirps out.

I hold my chuckle in. This girl. I swear. I follow her orders, letting her do her business. I'm surprised when she tells me I can turn back around that she's managed to get her outfit back into place. She perches up on her tiptoes and turns on the faucet, then runs her hand under the motion-censored soap dispenser.

She beams at me in the mirror as she rubs her tiny hands together while singing a tune I don't recognize. She doesn't ask for help reaching a paper towel. Nope, she jumps up and down waving her arm until the motion sensor detects movement and spills out towels.

"Ready to go." She tosses the paper towel in the trash can, twirls, and plops her hands on her hips.

I follow her out to her bag. I pick it up, ignoring all the stares as I follow Whit to my truck.

"Daddy."

"Yeah, Squirt?" I hoist her up in her booster seat.

She giggles. "I like that nickname. Can it be mine now?"

I shrug. "Sure, Squirt."

She giggles louder. "But I was going to ask can we go get ice cream?"

She latches her tiny hands in front of her chest in a praying motion and flattens out her lips.

"I don't think your mom would approve."

"Please, Daddy." She shakes her hands in front of her while pleading with her beautiful eyes.

I lean down and whisper in her ear. "Sure, it will be our secret, Squirt."

She begins kicking her feet in front of her. "Yes! I'm getting three scoops, sprinkles, and the white fluffy stuff."

I bite on my bottom lip and grab the back of my neck. I have a pretty damn good hunch this is going to get my ass in trouble.

Chapter 13

Jules

"We need to talk." Jessie rounds the corner of the barn.

I freeze with the tip of the lit cigarette at my lips. His footsteps stutter for a brief second, but then he continues to walk right up to me.

"Didn't know you took up smoking," he mumbles, placing his hands on his hips.

I shrug. It's a celebratory smoke. Became my tradition after the first thoroughly edited book I sent off to my publisher. I'd craved the temporary high from the nicotine. Not that I was ever an addicted smoker, but back in my high school days, we'd have a few while drinking. I forced myself only to indulge when I'd sent off a book because it could quickly become a habit.

I inhale deeply on the cigarette, letting it settle in before turning my head and exhaling. Jessie remains in front of me shocked as shit. It is quite comical and ruins my goal of relaxing on a high for a few brief seconds. His presence has been dangerous since the morning we all woke up together in bed. I haven't slept that well in years, and that sensation itself could become addictive. I pulled back, distanced myself, but never once pulled Whit away from him. I'll never do that to him and, more importantly, her.

"I don't smoke," I offer.

He quirks an eyebrow up in question then leans back on the barn, crossing his arms over his broad chest and rolling his face to stare at me.

"It's complicated. Don't judge." I bring the end of the cigarette to my lips and inhale deeply once again.

"Not judging. Just shocked."

I flutter my eyes shut, exhaling, feeling my limbs relax, then I reach down and grab my glass of wine and take a long drink, the other piece of my simple celebratory tradition that I indulge in.

"So, what do we need to talk about?" I lean my shoulder on the barn, dropping my head to the hardwood then staring into his rich, whiskey-colored eyes.

Jessie doesn't break eye contact as he reaches down for my wine glass and brings it to his lips. His jaw tightens, and the expanse of his neck moves with the motion. His lips on my wine glass make my insides clench. The memories of his mouth on mine are powerful and threatening to overtake my common sense. The action is erotic and stimulating, making my knees weaken.

His manly scent attacking me doesn't help matters. Neither do his bulging biceps peeking out of his black V-neck t-shirt. Another few glasses of wine and I'd be tearing off his clothes, damn the consequences, just to have his naked body pressed into mine one more time. The protection of safety and love he used to pour my direction would satisfy all my cravings for him. It would be a mistake, and thank God I haven't had any more wine than I have already consumed.

It's a fact the heart loves who the heart loves. There's no denying it. I've never quit loving this man and never will. I'm not ready to admit it to anyone. I internally wince, remembering the time I told him. I don't know if I'll ever be brave enough to say it out loud again. I may have to settle for loving him from a distance. And even that would be worth it, or that's what I keep telling myself.

Jessie hands me the glass before speaking. "Whit. She had a meltdown today at the football field."

This snaps me out of my drunken-induced Jessie haze. "And you're just telling me?"

I know I snap at him and can't help it. Whit and Jessie have been home for three hours; we all sat down to a home-cooked meal of fried chicken and chatted. Whit didn't eat much, which I thought was odd because there was a bowl of olives on the table. I should've known something was wrong. I internally beat myself up for being a shit mom.

"Calm down." He reaches out, grabbing my hand. I don't pull away, letting the warmth of his contact comfort me. He looks out to the pasture, raking his other hand through his hair. "She melted down over football and the fact you hate it. She equated it to me not having time for her."

My chest heaves with a heavy burden and pain for my little girl. I never kept it a secret from anyone that I hated the sport. And it's obvious why. That damn sport took everything away from me. It detoured my future onto a different path I never saw coming. Even though it wasn't planned, I wouldn't change it for the world because of my girl.

"I never told her," I whispered.

I'm not sure if he heard me or not. My hand trembles as I grab the wine glass and bring it to my lips. The once-sweet wine has now turned bitter, gliding down the back of my throat.

After swallowing, I continue to talk. It's raw and honest. The time for fluffy fillers expired a long time ago. Jessie has rolled his head to stare my way once again.

"I hate football. I saw it as the one factor that took you away from me. I've never been able to stomach the sport." I keep my gaze down on my toes peeking out of my sandals. "But I never told Whit a thing except that you were a busy person. I never once told her the whole story. I'm human, though, and had to release emotions somehow."

"I get it, Jules." He squeezes my hand. "You don't have to explain yourself to me. I just wanted to let you know about it. I reassured her once again."

"Thank you," I whisper.

"I guess while we're talking about today, I should also tell you that she overheard me cussing out a player and we had ice cream before dinner."

I snap my head up to stare at him, shake my hand

away from his, and stab my finger in his chest. "That's why she didn't eat any dinner."

Jessie's cheeks actually heat up to a shade of red. "Yeah, that's my bad."

"This is weird," I blurt out.

That's when he jerks me out in front of him. Before I know it, he's guiding me down to the pond. It's not any luxurious pond, but a damn irrigation pond. I follow him only because his skin glides against mine and that slight high I was craving lingers behind. I know damn well Whit is cuddled up next to Nana. And both of them are passed out. Whit barely made it through dinner, and Nana has been exhausted since the service.

"I don't think it is," he replies, gently squeezing my hand.

"Uh?" I ask, craning my neck to look at him. I've forgotten what we were talking about.

He stops on the edge of the pond. The place we used to watch the sunset every single night back in high school. Jessie grabs my other hand, tugging me to his chest. He doesn't stop there, pulling me to his chest and wrapping his arms low around my waist.

"You said it's weird. It's not. I feel like I'm finally home even though I've been here a few years." He pauses, kissing the top of my head. "This is so damn surreal, Jules."

"It's something," I mumble into his chest.

"Thank you for allowing me this. I know we have a lot of shit to work on and you very well could've kept me blocked out, but you didn't." He exhales loudly. "I keep waiting to wake up from this dream."

"It's not a dream." I nestle my cheek into his chest, inhaling his scent. My heart thunders against my sternum. A herd of bulls stampedes through every emotion. "Tell me about it."

He takes a step back, peering down at me with confusion dancing in his rich chocolate eyes.

I mirror his movements, tucking my arms at my sides and ducking my chin. I'm not sure why I'm asking. It must be a rare form of self-torture similar to the nights I'd Google search his name. I only did it a few times because the fit of tears was never worth it.

"Tell me about college. I want to know everything." I step toward the pond.

The only way I know he's following me is from the sound of the tall, crisp pasture grass trailing behind me. Jessie remains silent for long beats. I find the old worn log we used to cuddle on. The flattened surface remains upwards to the heavens, making it perfect for sitting. I sit down and wait for Jessie. He moves slowly and precisely as he sits next to me.

His elbows land heavily on the tops of his thighs, and he buries his face in his palms and lets out another gust of air. I reach over without thinking and squeeze his leg.

"We're here now, Jessie, and yes, it's weird as hell to me. You know what I've been up to since high school. I want to know everything you've done."

"This hurts like hell." His voice comes out in a growled whisper.

I don't say a word, giving him the silence he

needs. I'm not sure if he'll open up or keep the regret and hurt inside. Hell, I know it's the most natural thing to do. Way fucking easier than forgiving and moving on. I'm chalking it up to the fact life is short, and you have to cherish all of your days because you never know what could happen.

"Left a few days after graduation. I knew it was a mistake the moment I boarded the plane. It all felt so wrong without you, Jules. Then the proverbial carrot was dangled in front of my face, and I went for it. Campus life was wild. College ball and practice was nothing like high school. Pushed my body hard every single day. Started my freshman year and everything was perfect."

His chest heaves as each sentence flows from him. My heart hurts for him. I know it shouldn't if our past means anything to me and the endless nights I stayed awake crying, rocking a screaming newborn. The vision of Whit and Jessie happy together erases all of it. I'm left with only compassion for the man. Jessie continues telling me everything, not leaving out the college party scene or even his last game where he was taken out.

"Then I came home, and everything else fell into place. The head coach job opened up at the high school, and I didn't even have to interview for it." He swivels to face me. "Jules, not one fucking day has gone by where I didn't regret my decision and missed you like mad. You know the rest about me pestering your papa for your number and the whole Shayna deal."

"How serious was it with her?" I ask, not knowing why. I already know the answer, but it seems my dumb heart needs reassurance.

"Not proud of it, but I finally caved into the pressure from the town and Shayna's ruthless tactics. I never loved her."

I snort and shake my head. "You had to have some feelings for her."

"I tried, Jules, I sure in the hell did try, but there hasn't been anyone else but you. It's always been you."

I finally look up to him, nibbling on my lower lip for a few beats before speaking. "I'm not sure I can do this, Jessie, but the thing is I've never stopped loving you, and I hate you for that some days. My life is up in the air right now. All I can give you is one day at a time."

He slings his arm over my shoulder and tugs me to him. I melt into his side. "I'll take it."

We remain silent, watching the sun sink lower, to right before it kisses the horizon. Hues of pinks and oranges flash across the sky.

"Remember you used to say…"

I finish his sentence with him, "…the warmest color."

I pry my stare from the brilliance of God's miracle and right into Jessie's deep, rich and loving eyes. The glow from the setting sun illuminates his face. This time I'm the one to initiate the kiss. Our lips glide against each other, remembering the feel before I deepen the kiss. I glide my tongue along the seam of his lips until he parts for me. I groan into him as his taste assaults me. I'm lost in everything Jessie.

Chapter 14

Jessie

It's almost picture perfect. Damn close. I walked Jules up to the front door last night. Wanted nothing more than to kiss the hell out of her right then and there. Took everything inside of me not to. She squeezed my hand before dropping it then perched up on her tiptoes, pecking me on the cheek. The hunger and desire in her eyes nearly cracked me. The moments of silence we shared at the pond were a promise of old wounds healing. It gave me all the strength to push on.

I slam the steering wheel, overwhelmed and excited as hell. Whit decided to spend time with my mom this morning instead of going to football practice with me. I was totally fine with it since there's no way in hell I'll ever be able to control my colorful language. The raw emotions and my competitive side get me every single time when it comes to football.

Jules had no problems with Whit hanging out

down the road at my childhood home. Jane had errands to run, and Jules said she had to work. I opened my mouth to ask about it, but Jules' expression conveyed it wasn't open for discussion. When I hinted around with questions, Whit only shrugged and told me her momma works a lot on her computer and sometimes even stays up all night long on it.

Frustration builds low in my abdomen, threatening to erupt over the fact there's so much I don't know about her. *Baby steps*, I keep reminding myself. That's what it's going to take to make this all possible.

A smile covers my face as I cut the engine in the driveway. Whit is covered from head to toe in dirt with patches of mud covering her kneecaps peeking out underneath a tutu. She clutches an overflowing basket of tomatoes to her chest. The moment she spots my old truck, the tomatoes shower up in air as she drops the basket and bolts to me. I hustle out of the truck. She's at my door leaping up in the air before I have a chance to take a step toward her.

"Daddy!" She wraps her arms around my neck as I hoist her up to my sweaty chest. We're quite the stinky, dirty duo, and I wouldn't have it any other way. This girl is all mine in so many damn ways. "Did you see all those tomatoes, Daddy?"

I chuckle, the vibration thick in my chest. "I sure did."

She pulls back, staring me in the eyes. "We are gonna make salads, salsa, and jam with them."

I peer over her shoulder to see my mom with happy tears brimming in her eyes and a contagious smile whispering on her lips.

"Sounds like you had fun with…"

Whit wiggles out my arms before I have the chance to finish my sentence. She's on the ground and sprinting back towards the empty basket framed by plump, red tomatoes.

"Grandma!" Whit slides on the grass, swooping her arms out to scoop back up the produce. "I got them."

Well, shit, that one word gutted me hard. I've been selfish since the day Whit told me she didn't talk to strangers. I felt robbed and pissed off more than ever at myself for my selfish and ridiculous decision. I stole joy, happiness, and love from everyone in my life.

The front door to my childhood home creaks open. Jules steps out with a frosted pitcher of what looks to be lemonade. She tucks a stray curl behind her ear and then ruffles the messy bun on top of her head before she looks up. The exhausted sun has just begun its descent to slumber, cascading an illuminating glow on her features. The stress, exhaustion, and grieving have all disappeared in the winds of the cooling summer evening.

A smile lights up her face as she watches Whit finishing the task of scooping up the tomatoes with my mom at her side. Whit hasn't stopped rattling on about canning, slicing, and selling tomatoes for big money to notice her mom on the porch. I clear my throat, catching Jules' attention. A genuine smile stays placed on her face. At this moment, I have no doubt my future indeed began.

"Jessie." She jerks her chin then tucks her hands

in the pockets of her too goddamn short shorts while sauntering down the front steps.

My cock stirs in my gym shorts. Not a good combination. I see this woman in a whole different light. She's not the once-gangly eleven year old or the fit and toned high school senior. No, she's so much more. Curves and flesh that created my daughter. Her body plump to perfection in all the right spots. Her luscious tits bounce under her white tank top. And now I have a full-fledged hard on. I pull my attention away from her and study the ground, making my way to her. I focus on the funky smell and nasty sights from my years in locker rooms to wish the boner away.

"Hey." Her sweet voice drifts across the crisp air.

I glance up to see Jules shading her eyes with that contagious smile still painting her face.

"Hey, you." I jerk my chin and then massage the back of my neck. I have to do something with my hand, so I don't pull her into a heated kiss that wouldn't stop with just kissing.

"Came up here to check on Whit and, well, just stayed here. Hope you don't mind." Our knuckles brush as we saunter up to the porch.

I glance over at her profile, admiring the tender tanned skin of her neck, wanting nothing more than to lick every square inch of the sweetness. "You should know the answer to that question."

When I'm just feet within the front porch, her MacBook comes into view on the table. My curiosity piques, but I find myself tamping it down and taking a seat on the first step instead. Jules glides up the steps, settling in the worn rocking chair in front of her laptop.

"Mommy." Whit skips up to the steps. "Do you have the lemonade done for my stand?"

Whit scrambles up into my lap, lacing her arms around my neck and resting her chin on the top of my shoulder, facing her mom.

"Honey, I told you I'd make lemonade for you. Nobody will be by here to buy it. We could do a lemonade party like a tea party."

"Momma," she whines. "Please. Grandma helped me make a sign, and she said we could set up a table by the driveway."

Mom steps up to us with a worried look on her face. I know exactly how she's feeling. This is all so new, and the last thing any of us want to do is overstep boundaries and spook Jules away.

"Whit, lemonade stands only work in busy areas."

"Not in that book you read me last week. Remember the kids lived in the country and they made one hundred nineteen dollars."

"Whit, that was fiction."

Without turning around, I can hear the clicking of fingers on a keyboard and know Jules is multi-tasking right now. Whit isn't giving up.

"Hey." I smooth down her hair. "Go get that sign set up and get your lemonade over there on the picnic table under the oak tree. But your mom is right. There isn't much traffic on this road, so don't get disappointed if you don't sell any."

"Yes. Yes. Yes." Whit hops off my lap and squeals all the way up the steps.

Mom helps her pack out the large pitcher of lemonade. Whit buzzes up and down the sidewalk and porch bringing out the sign, cups, pens, papers, and a small wooden box.

Whit clambers up the picnic table and plops on the top with her feet dangling on the part you're supposed to sit on. Mom settles next to her feet and does her best to brush away the dried mud and dirt.

"Grandma, thank you so much. This is my biggest dream ever come true." Whit leans down, doing her version of whispering which, in all reality, is her normal voice.

"Jessie."

I turn and kick my feet up on the porch, leaning back on the railing. Lengthening my spine and stretching my arms over my head relaxes all of my sore muscles. Growing older is kicking my ass. I do my best to workout with my team. I do everything they do, always believing that modeling is the best way to learn.

"Yeah," I respond, not missing the fact Jules' vision lingered a bit too long on the sliver of my exposed abs. I decide to keep my hands high above my head.

"You do realize one day that you'll have to tell her no."

"Says who?" I smirk.

Jules shakes her head and snaps the lid of her MacBook shut. "The universe. It's part of being a parent."

"I've always been known to break a few rules and exceed all expectations." I'm forced to drop my arms from the growing tingling in the tips of my fingers.

"I'll have a tissue and a case of beer ready for you when the day comes." She stands up and walks over to me. I swing my legs back down to the steps and wait for her to take a seat.

"Will you also rub my back and cuddle me until I feel better?" I bump her shoulder with mine.

She snorts. And hell do I get throttled back into the past. Jules always hated her snort when she laughed, but I thought it was cute as hell.

"I'm serious, Jessie." She bumps my shoulder right back. "Parenting isn't easy and really, really sucks when you have to be the bad guy. It won't always be like this."

She waves her hand in front of her. I grab it and link our fingers together, doing my best to soothe the silent worry away. I get where she's going with this, and by damn I do feel like it's a small victory that we're communicating about this. Also, I know her skeptical concerns and worry won't diminish anytime soon.

"I hear ya, Jules, and I've coached enough kids to know the heartache that goes with it. Will keep saying it and showing you until you believe it…I'm not going anywhere. I'm in this for the long haul. That means all of the yes and no moments."

"You were always a smooth talker, Jessie."

"Yeah, thinking our baby girl acquired the trait from me." My shoulders loosen when Jules lays her head on top of them.

"Daddy!" Whit shades her eyes and looks our direction then bounds our way. I don't miss her vision raking over our interlocked hands. She doesn't stumble over a word, though. "You want a lemonade?"

"Sure do." I wink at her.

She climbs up the first step, places one hand on my knee, and then plops out her other palm. "That'll be two dollars."

"Two dollars?" I scrunch my brows. "That's a bit steep, and don't I get the family discount?"

"Nope." She pops the "p" and stares me down. "Grandma said I can't give anyone a break, and that's damn good lemonade, well worth two dollars."

Mom clears her throat from behind Whit. Whit covers her mouth and giggles.

"Oops…I wasn't supposed to say that part."

I dig into the pockets of my gym shorts and pull out my worn leather wallet I've carried since high school, producing a five-dollar bill and handing it over to her. Jules clears her throat next to me, and I glance towards her. She spotted the picture in my wallet, the same one that's been there for years. It's worn, and its corners are tattered up a bit. But it's her. It's my favorite picture of her down at the pond with a fishing pole in her hand and a smile that could light up the darkest of days. It got me through so damn many of them.

Whit plucks the bill from my hand. "One lemonade coming up."

She races off with my mom on her heels. The two chatter away and giggle the entire time. A thick wave of awkwardness drifts between Jules and me. She hasn't pulled back from my body, but mentally I need to give her time. I pull my cell from my pocket and fire off a text to the guys telling them they'd better get their ass over here and buy some lemonade.

"Here you go." Whit hands me the clear plastic cup of lemonade with its contents sloshing over the sides. "Oh, and Grandma told me to tell you we don't have change."

I shoot up an eyebrow. "A five-dollar lemonade? This better be delicious, little girl."

I poke at her ribs, hating missing the contact of Jules' hand as I bring the cup to my lips. I've had this same lemonade for years. Not going to lie, Mom makes a mean one and even back in the day shared her recipe with Jules. But at this moment, it's the sweetest and best goddamn lemonade I've ever had.

Whit's head whips around when she hears an engine.

"Might be customers," my mom hollers from the table holding the drinks.

Whit buzzes off the steps, darting down the sidewalk.

"Do not go outside of that gate," Jules hollers from beside me.

Whit stomps her foot but listens to her mom, all the while waving down the vehicle pulling in the front.

Before Brady and Tessi can climb out of their vehicle, Whit is already giving them the pitch.

"How?" Jules whispers.

I drain the rest of the most expensive lemonade I've ever bought and turn to her. Without thinking, I lean over and kiss her temple, letting my lips linger a bit too long on her sweet skin. "I called in the cavalry for my girl."

Tessi hollers out Jules' name and waves. A long line of old beat-up trucks and cars pull in behind Brady.

"How in the hell do you know this many people?" she asked, astonished, resting her head back on my shoulder.

"They are my boys. Sent a group text telling them they'd better get their asses down here and buy lemonade." I reach over, running the pad of my finger down her jawline, unable to help myself.

"And they just hop when you snap?" she asks, her eyes fluttering shut. The long, thick eyelashes flicker on her tender skin.

I back up, knowing we are about to be bombarded and I'm not ready to deal with inquisitive stares and a hundred questions. "Told them they didn't have to run tomorrow if they did so."

The serenading of engines cutting off and doors slamming shut fill the front yard. Tessi grabs Jules from the front steps and wraps her up in a hug. Brady shoots me a look that I ignore. He's been on my ass about me getting in too deep. It's not that he doesn't love Jules. It's more of him not wanting to see his best friend, who's more like a brother, hit rock bottom once again.

The thing is I'm not losing this battle. I'm the underdog and will fight with everything I have to right all my wrongs even if it takes me under.

"Coach!" Max Statton jogs up to me.

The young boy won me over the day he walked

to practice in a worn-out pair of tennis shoes, jeans, and a tank top. The rest of the team gave him hell. It was a battle to keep my arms crossed over my chest and watch the tryouts. Brinkley, the junior high gym teacher and basketball coach, showed up twenty minutes later with a pair of gym shorts for him.

Max gave her a hug and changed into them, and from that moment on, he has shut up the entire team with drive and talent. I'm going to piss off the entire community when I slot him in as a starter as a freshman on the varsity team. He has no big name in this small, one-horse town. His mom is a drunk and hardly ever home. Talked to a few elementary teachers to only find out he's had one shitty life but has never given up.

A few juniors have taken him under their wing. I'm still skeptical if they're genuine or setting him up for a prank.

"Max." I stand up and hold my arms open, giving him a man hug.

"Heard they're selling lemonade around here." He steps back, running his hand through his hair.

"Sure are."

"Whit?" he asks.

I nod.

"Got paid today and pretty damn thirsty." He smirks.

"How's it going over at Gravy Dave's?" I ask, wishing more than hell he could have a better job. The kid would be a damn good farm hand. Jules' Papa is the only man in these parts who would hire him. He never gave a damn about social classes and all that other shit.

"It sucks." He shrugs. "But I'm getting paid. Had enough this month to pay rent and get the power turned back on."

My teeth grind together, causing my jaw to cramp in a fucking rage. The longer I've known Max, the more he's opened up to me. But this bit of information is about to throttle me over the fucking edge.

"Hey," Jules' sweet voice interrupts. "I don't think I've met you."

Max blushes right before me. I stifle a chuckle. The little shit is struck by her beauty.

"I'm—uh…Max."

Jules holds out her hand, and he reacts in slow motion. "Nice to meet you. You play football for this fool here?"

Max's blush deepens. The poor boy is about to pass out any minute. "Yes, ma'am, but he isn't a…"

Jules throws her head back in laughter. "Oh, Max, you need to hang out with me a bit, and you can figure out this one."

"Oh-kay," he responds.

"My nana needs some extra help moving water and keeping up her place. Why don't you stop by when you have time? I know you're a busy kid, so let me know if you have time." She taps his shoulder.

Max nods. "Yes, ma'am."

"It's Jules, Max." She winks at him.

He nods again, his hands shaking at his sides. "Gonna buy some lemonade now."

He rushes off to the group of his teammates swarmed around Whit's stand. An arm wraps low around my waist, and the sweet, tender smell of lilac and grapefruit attacks my senses.

"How did you know I was about to break?" I whisper.

"Can read you like a book, Jessie, even after all these years." She squeezes my side. "And I'm pretty sure you've made your daughter's year."

We both watch the action over at the lemonade stand. My chest tightens when Max whips out his wallet and hands over a five-dollar bill then proceeds to wave off his change.

"No, pretty sure she made my year," I whisper to no one and everyone at the same time.

Chapter 15

Jules

"Momma." Whit waves the empty lemonade pitcher for the fifth time.

"I'll get it." Jessie lays his hand on the top of my thigh as he gets up and jogs down to our daughter.

Our daughter still sounds foreign on my tongue. I'm distracted watching those loose gym shorts flow around his thick thighs that lead up to his waist. His damn cut-off workout t-shirt only taunts me. It was the passion he showed when one of his players displayed a struggle that gutted me. Jessie has put his heart and soul into this team, all the time waiting for me to come back. I know beyond a doubt he's been here waiting on me. It's evident in his voice and from the stories Nana and Tessi have shared with me.

The one thing I'm struggling to get over is the fact he was with Shayna. In the back of my head, I get it. I truly do. I've always known how this town shone a light on Jessie. They were encouraging his next step. He had no way of contacting me, and he let her go the moment he knew I was back. All of it sounds perfect. Except for that little reminder in the back of my head screaming at me and reminding me he dumped me the moment something bigger came by years ago as well.

"Jules." Someone shakes my shoulder.

"What's up?" I turn to Tessi, trying to act like I haven't missed a beat of our conversation.

"I've asked you what your plans are four times while you've stared out in the distance."

"Plans?" I pivot in the rocking chair to face her.

She swallows hard before speaking. "Are you going back to California?"

I shrug. And in all honesty, it's the best damn answer I have. I know I can't leave my nana, yet some hours of the day I want to run away from all the feelings, and California is that safe harbor for me.

"I'm just taking it day by day, seeing how Nana is coping. I'm able to work from home for now." I begin gently rocking.

The front screen door swings open, and Jessie walks out with a pitcher of lemonade. He stops for a moment and kisses the top of my head before jutting off. The line of customers begins to dwindle with only a handful of players waiting on their lemonade.

"What's going on, Jules?" Genuine concern floats in each word of her question.

I let out a long breath of air. "Honestly, Tessi, I have no damn idea. My anger is changing into something I'm not sure I'll be able to digest. It's a foreign feeling to have it all dissipate after years of living with it."

"Can I say something?" She reaches over and squeezes my hand, interrupting me. She doesn't wait for me to say yes before going on. "You belong here. I have no idea what your life was like in California, but you and Whit are a part of this town. I can't imagine how scary it must be to believe in happiness again or even try to, but you deserve it. And Jules, look at that girl. She's so damn happy."

I nod, unable to speak a word. Tessi lightens the conversation, talking about her kids and that we need to have a playdate. Soon enough, the dusk of the evening settles and blesses us with a beautiful glow. The last truck pulls out of the drive, leaving only Brady's rig behind.

"Mom!" Whit runs up to the steps, waving a Ziploc bag of cash in front of her. "Look at this."

She plops down on the porch, pinches open the bag with her tiny fingers, and begins stacking all the bills. Not a single one-dollar bill is in the mix. I shake my head at the ridiculousness. I don't have the energy to scold Jessie over it, because quite frankly, I'm relaxed and enjoying the moment. Starting a new novel is never easy and seems to zap all of my energy and brainpower, so this is perfect right now.

Jessie and Brady haul the table back to the shed while Jessie's mom sits down next to Whit, helping her count the money.

"I know how to count by fives, Grandma." Whit brushes her bangs from her face.

The men join us, coming from inside the house out on the porch. The red Solo cups in their hands make me shake my head. After dumping the table, they snuck in the back door to make a cocktail. It reminds me of the days we used to sneak into Jessie's dad's booze cabinet. Hell, all of our parents had their booze stolen by us in our high school years.

Brady nudges Tessi up out of her seat, carefully balancing his drink in his hand, and then plops right down. Seconds later, he tugs her down in his lap. She curls right up into his chest. My heart pangs with hurt and longing. It had only been a fantasy to have that in my life the last several years, and now I'm sitting here faced with it possibly being a reality.

Jessie squeezes the top of my shoulder, leans down, and hands me the cup. I don't think twice about taking a drink. The sweet taste of Jack Daniels and Coke goes down easy, adding to my relaxed state.

"One day that'll be us," he whispers in my ear.

I take another drink, hoping it would ease the pressure building up in my core. My body is on fire for Jessie. It's a burn that's only increasing and not simmering out.

"Ninety, one hundred." Whit shakes her head. "Five…"

"Here, sweet bug." Carolyn grabs the stack of money that equals one hundred. "Now start back at five."

The two go back to it. Whit has to stop and start a few times because of her excitement.

"I can't believe she can count by fives already," Tessi says.

"Yeah, no shit," Brady adds. "Lenny can't do that, and he's a year older than her."

I wave him off. "She's always been curious and soaked everything up at preschool. They moved her up a few classes because she'd get so bored."

Jessie relaxes on the table next to me. "It's not the preschool, Jules; it's because you've done a damn incredible job with her."

He rests his hand on the top of my thigh. My gaze darts to Brady and Tessi to measure their reaction. I'm shocked when they don't blink twice. The warmth from his touch fires me up even more. In a bold move, I reach down and cover his hand with mine. Desire and comfort coat me in a gentle hug. The sensation fills and overwhelms me at the same time.

Whit jumps up on her feet. "One hundred eighty-five dollars, and Momma, you said nobody would stop."

I smile and shake my head. "Luck was on your side, little one."

She climbs up into my lap, doing her best to nestle herself between Jessie and me. She's perched on the arm of the rocking chair after Jessie moved his arm to wrap it around my shoulders.

"I think it was Grandma's lemonade and Daddy telling his players they'd better get their a-s-s-es out here." She hugs the bag of cash to her chest.

We all erupt in laughter. I kiss the top of her head, taking a moment to inhale the sweet coconut scent of her shampoo.

"Can't get anything past you, now can we?" Jessie bends down and kisses her cheek.

"You kids want to stay for dinner?" Carolyn asks, standing up and brushing off her pants.

"Yes!" Whit squeals. "Can I help you cook?"

"Sure can, sweet bug." She smiles gently. "Brady, Ṭessi, have you eaten? Have some ribs ready to grill up."

"We haven't. Had planned on a date night until we got the 911 text from Jessie," Tessi announces.

"Even had a babysitter. You owe me, man," Brady growls.

"How about I get you all fed then you can go out?"

"We'd love that, Carolyn. Thank you." Tessi smacks Brady's chest.

Whit hops off my lap and freezes before following her grandma into the front door.

"Two things." She holds up two fingers, keeping her bag clutched to her chest with her other hand. "I'm gonna buy a puppy with this money, and Daddy, will you do the talent show with me that your players were talking about?"

I clear my throat, nearly falling out of the rocker. She's been begging for a puppy for almost a year now. It was never an option in California since where we lived didn't allow pets. Not to mention the fact I haven't had the time to take care of an extra body.

"Whit," I warn her. "You know we've discussed this."

She tilts her head, determination sparking in her rich brown eyes. "But we now can have dogs where we live, and I'll buy everything and take care of it every second."

"We will talk about it." I lean back in my chair, deciding to go with a pacifying comment instead of an outright battle after such a beautiful day and in front of friends and family.

"Yes, I get one." She punches the air.

Oh, the joys of reasoning with a five year old. It's a losing battle that has the power to irritate the hell out of you.

"And Daddy, will you dance with me at the local talent show?" She taps her temple. "I think it's on August something."

Jessie grimaces. The look on his face is downright comical. I bite my lip to stifle the laughter threatening to burst out. The ball is in his court, and I know there's no way in hell he'll tell his little girl no. And there's also the fact dancing in a talent show is the last thing he'd ever want to do.

"Yeah, we'll look into it." He nods.

With all of Whit's concerns appeased, she marches in the house, following her grandma. Once the screen door slams shut and Whit's chatter fades off, Brady busts a gut.

"Dude, that little girl has you wrapped around her pinky finger. Never thought I'd see the day that brooding, grumpy-ass Jessie would be a big ol' softy."

Tessi slaps him in the chest again. "Take it easy on him."

I grab the drink from Jessie's hand, sipping on it and loving the taste of the whiskey. It's just the right mix.

"And it's going to be a hard no on the dog," I say over the brim of the cup.

"She's right, though," Jessie adds, standing up and stretching.

"Don't you dare!" I point at him.

"Her points were very valid." He grins down at me. "Anyone else want another drink?"

"Jessie, I mean it," I scold.

His chuckle echoes on the porch, and I know I'm screwed in the dog war. I have no backup.

Chapter 16

Jessie

Fuck yes. A puppy would be the perfect fixture in hopes of keeping my girls here in Boone.

"Be good and no more s'mores, baby girl." Jules leans down and kisses Whit's forehead.

I do the same, then ruffle Whit's hair before we leave the backyard. Brady and Tessi hop in their truck. Jules and I do the same thing, hopping in mine. There's an awkward moment of silence once we are both settled in. I fire up the engine, wanting nothing more than to snag Jules' thigh and drag her over to me. I grip the steering wheel, keeping my hands in a safe zone.

I pop the truck into reverse, peering over my shoulder, easing it out on the dirt road. I hear then feel the movement of Jules sliding right over to the center. Her body presses against mine. I take a moment to control my breathing before facing the road.

I drop my arm to the top of her thigh, giving it a

gentle squeeze, hoping to convey my gratitude for whatever she's giving me.

I clear my throat before speaking. "You do know between our two moms that Whit will more than likely eat at least five more s'mores."

Jules groans. "I know."

Jane joined us for dinner along with my dad. We all enjoyed some great laughs and even better food. It was Brady's idea to head out to Cody's bar. Jules and I never stood a chance to turn down the offer. My parents practically shoved me out the door, and Jane did the same thing to Jules. They had no problem doting on Whit.

"Was that hard?" I ask, turning onto the paved road. "Leaving her."

I catch the motion out of the corner of my eye of her shaking her head. "No, not at all, actually. It's weird because I only left Whit with my best friend, Lydia, back in California, and I could probably count the times on one hand. It's just a new feeling, you know."

"I can't imagine." I squeeze her thigh. "Damn proud of you. I know it can't be easy with all of this new stuff."

She laces her hand in mine. Years ago, it was her favorite thing to do. You'd find Jules clutched to my hand wherever we were. It takes me back. Damn, it feels freaking amazing, and it's the one thing I'm choosing to focus on.

"Thank you, Jessie." She leans her head on my shoulder. "That was pretty amazing what you did with your player, Max."

"Yeah, he has a shit life, and the team hasn't

been so nice to him. Takes everything for me not to knock them on their asses, but it wouldn't do a damn thing for him. He has to find his way." I pull the truck to a stop at a sign and peer down at her. "Thank you for extending that offer for him. Not much has changed in this small, judgmental town. He'd be one hell of a farm hand, but no one wanted to hire him because of his mom and his last name."

"Papa would've in a heartbeat," she whispers.

"Yes, he would've and guarantee you he's smiling from up there for what you did with him."

We make the rest of the drive to Cody's bar in the neighboring town in silence. It's neither uncomfortable nor deafening with fear. It's a new promise of the future that makes us high as hell on life.

When I pull into the bar's parking lot, it's packed as usual. The feeling of exhilaration is threatening to deflate. There will be prying stares. The thing about Cody's bar is that everyone from surrounding towns claims it as their watering hole. It's just one more obstacle I'll have to overcome because of my choices from years past and one I'll face head-on with no doubt.

"Jessie." Jules' voice drifts in the cab once I find a parking spot and kill the engine.

"Yeah." I shift in my seat to face her.

She fiddles with her fingers on the hem of her shorts. She's nibbling on her bottom lip, avoiding eye contact. I have no idea what she's about to drop on me, but I'm confident she's nervous as hell about it.

I grab her hands, holding them in one of mine,

then tilt her chin up to me with my pointer finger. "Say it, baby."

Her eyelids flutter shut. "If you want to pick me up out of my seat tonight and then set me in your lap, I wouldn't mind."

Her chest heaves with each word, and no doubt in my mind might be the hardest thing she's ever had to say to me. I lean down and kiss her forehead, not saying another word before I open the door to my truck. I slide out, keeping hold of her hand and tugging her to the edge of the seat.

I face her until her legs dangle on my side. My arms go on automatic, wrapping around her ass, bringing her closer to me. Jules gasps, planting her hands on the tops of my shoulders.

"Remember this?" I ask, crooking my head.

"Yes." Jules drops her head to mine. "Same truck, too."

"Could never sell it. Too many damn memories live in it, and I hoped like hell one day your scent would be back in it."

"And we're here," she whispers.

"Remember the day old Pence chased us out of the parking lot after school when she caught us nearly rounding third base in this position?"

Jules throws her head back, barking out a loud bout of laughter. "Oh my God, that was horrible and so damn embarrassing. Both of our parents were waiting for us on the porch by the time we got home."

I shake my head. "I still can't look that old bat in the eyes. She still makes me feel like that teenage boy caught with his hand in the cookie jar."

Jules' arms go from my shoulders to wrap around my neck, and she sinks down on the seat until we are chest to chest. "I'm scared, and it's not about loving you but about everyone else and their stares and judgement. We've done okay so far protecting Whit from it, but you know it's coming."

"That's on me. Do you hear me?" I reach up and grip the back of her neck, bringing her lips to mine. Each word I speak is imprinted on her mouth. "It's because of what I did, and that's the shit I'll own to the world. Nobody, not even the goddamn mayor, will judge you or Whit. One word comes from a mouth, and their ass is mine. That's a fucking promise I'll never break."

"We are really doing this, aren't we?" she whispers into my lips.

"I'm all in, baby. It's your move."

Not another word is exchanged as she slides down to the ground and grabs my hand in hers. We walk hand in hand into the bar, and just as expected, the music is blaring and the temperature in the bar is excruciating. The garage door is open, doing its best to let in the fresh air of the evening. Brady and Tessi wave us down from a corner booth.

I jerk my head toward them as I weave through the droves of patrons. Jules keeps her hand clutched in mine with her other hand pressed low on my back. I may walk a bit slower than normal, loving the hell out of the feeling.

Cody has a leg hitched up on a chair with his infamous bar rag dangling out of his back pocket. He's in his signature black boots, white wife beater, and worn jeans. He follows Tessi's line of vision when we approach behind him.

"Well, som'bitch," Cody hollers out, pushes me out of the way, and wraps up Jules. "My girl came back for another taste of Cody."

I grab Jules by the waist, snarling at Cody. It only fuels his fire. He tosses his head back, howling in laughter. It's Cody's gig, and that's to get under everyone's skin as much as possible.

"Well, well, it seems things have changed since your last visit, Jules." He hitches his leg back up on the chair.

Jules relaxes back into my chest. My arms go on automatic, wrapping her up, resting my thumbs right above the button on her jeans. My dick kicks in protest against my zipper. Not sure if it's intentional or not, but Jules presses back on me.

"What's it to you?" Jules fires back.

Cody shakes his head. "Damn, and here I thought I had a chance even if it was a one-night stand."

I reach forward with one hand and thump him in the chest. "You're an asshole."

Cody goes on and on, laughing his ass off until his name is called out from the bar.

"I'll be right back over with your drinks. They're on the house tonight."

"No tequila," Jules hollers after him.

Cody doesn't stop his stride. He only raises an arm, shaking off the suggestion. Then he's distracted by a hot piece of ass. The man can't help himself and swats it and then kisses her on the cheek.

"He really hasn't changed, has he?" Jules asks,

taking a seat.

"Not a bit," I answer. "If anything, he may be getting worse."

"Yeah, he's declining back to a twelve-year-old boy who just learned about boners." Brady slaps the table. "Bastard better get our drinks over here and quick."

"I'll go make sure he stays focused." I bend down and kiss the top of Jules' head before weaving back through the crowd.

I hear my name shouted out several times on the way to the bar. We'd never get our drinks with how fucking packed this place is tonight. At this damn rate, Cody will be richer than any of us. The boy is making bank and couldn't be prouder of him. He notices me when I saddle up to the end of the bar. He gives me a jerk of the chin, letting me know he's making our drinks.

I do my best to keep my gaze focused on the worn surface of the bar top. Cody's Shaggin' Shack is burned into the wood with his infamous motto in smaller font below it: "Drink, Laugh, and Fuck."

"Jessie."

On instinct, I jerk up my head when I hear my name. It takes me three seconds to make eye contact with Shayna. She wasn't the one to call my name. No, it was the group of women surrounding her. The glass tumbler of whiskey perched on her lips instantly slams down on the bar. Her hand shakes as she grabs a bottle of water.

I grimace then do my best to cover it up. She'd been blowing up my phone so damn bad I was forced to block her number. She quit showing up at my house a few days ago. The crazy-ass woman would be sitting on my porch steps; who knows for how damn long at that? I've told her over and over how it's going to be. And she damn well knew we were on a rocky road before Jules showed back up in town.

A week before Jules returned, Shayna even admitted she knew I didn't love her and never would and that would be just fine with her. She'd deal with it, and all she wanted was a big diamond ring on her hand and my last name to sport around. She was even as blunt to tell me she wanted all of that by the time my team won the state title for the fourth time.

I drop my head and shake it back and forth, sick and pissed off at myself for settling for something like that. I was far off from marrying her, that's for damn sure, but doesn't make me any kind of respectable man to stay in an uncomfortable relationship.

"Here. Get the hell out of here before the bitch attacks." Cody slides across a tray filled with drinks. "You know I never did like that bitch."

I nod. "Yeah, I know. None of my friends did. Hey, what's this shit?"

I point to two large pitchers on the center of the tray.

"A Pussy Pleaser for my girl, Jules." He folds his arms over his chest with a crooked grin on his face.

"Idiot." I shake my head.

"She didn't tell you I pleased the hell out of her pussy the last time she was here." This time he cracks a mile-wide smile.

If there weren't a fifth of Jack Daniels on the tray, I'd reach over and smack him upside the head.

"Put it on my tab." I grab the tray and back quickly away from the bar.

That gains a hearty chuckle out of him. Brady and I both pay up our tabs every six months. Cody never keeps track, and hell, neither do we. We both end up hefting over around five hundred dollars. Who knows if it even comes close?

It's trickier than shit making it back to our table. The last shred of my patience frays when the fifth stumbling, drunk asshole knocks into my shoulder and some Pussy Pleaser splashes on my shirt.

"About damn time," Brady barks out.

"Don't even," I warn, gently putting the tray on the table. "That was fucking hell."

I pinch my shirt and pull it out, waving it in hopes it will dry. Sure as shit will stain with the vibrant red hue of the drink.

"Drinks!" Tessi claps her hands together, bouncing up and down in her seat. She could care less about my sour mood right now.

"You okay?" Jules asks, peering up at me.

I am now, I think to myself. My shoulders relax, and I remember why I'm here. Everything falls into place again. I wink down at her. She doesn't have a chance to react when I bend down to scoop her up in my arms and take her seat. I whirl her around in a quick motion, so she's sitting on my lap.

"Jessie," she squeals, keeping her arms wrapped around my neck until we settle in.

"Yeah," I murmur into her ear, wrapping my arms around her waist.

Fuck, I'd give anything to have her facing me, her luscious tits pressed into my chest and hot center lined up with my throbbing dick.

"Thank you," she whispers into my lips, letting them linger on mine. I wouldn't consider it quite a kiss, but it was something. And if that's all I get from this woman for the rest of my life, I'll drink it up.

"Pussy Pleasers," Tessi shouts over the thrumming music, catching all of our attention.

"Hey, don't drink it all." Jules adjusts herself in my lap, so she's facing the table and has one arm slung over my neck.

Brady goes about the task of pouring drinks for the girls then mixing a stiff drink for us. Jules grabs her glass then waits for the rest of us to follow suit. Brady goes to tip his back and is stopped when Jules shouts at him.

"Wait!" She holds up a hand. "A toast. We need to remember this moment forever."

She pauses, strumming her finger on the tabletop. We all wait for her; me, impatiently.

"Okay." She clears her throat and tightens her arm looped around my neck, so her side is pressed into my chest. She raises her glass, and we all follow suit until the crystal walls are all connected. "Coming home should be easy, or that's what they all say. It was the scariest thing I've ever done. A part of my heart that was dead started to slowly beat again the second I drove down the main street of Boone. I know yesterday is gone and I'm okay with that. I have a new future now. To my family, my friends, my love, and my hometown. Cheers!"

Brady and Tessi both holler out "cheers" in unison. I can't fucking manage to croak out the one simple word. Her words crushed and rejuvenated me all at the same time. There's no way I'll ever be able to process them. Jules blossomed, opening into a beautiful rose right in front of me. She put fear and anger aside to give the future just one glimpse of a chance. I'm finally able to rasp out the word.

We all bring our drinks to our lips and toss them back. Tessi continues with another toast. She pesters Brady until he caves into giving his own toast. I'm saved when Cody joins us. He drags a chair over to our table, whirls it backward, and takes a seat. He pours himself a Jack over ice.

I've never been so thankful to see the smartass in my life. There was no way in hell I'd be able to put together a toast that would do anything justice, and if I happened to, I'd cry right here in a bar. And it would have nothing to do with being tipsy.

The girls end up feeding the jukebox blasting all sorts of 80's and 90's jams, each and every one holding a long ago memory. And just like back in the day, we men stretched out our legs, relaxed back in our chairs, drank, bullshitted, and watched the girls dance their asses off. The only thing missing was the rusty tailgate of a truck.

"So, you two back together?" Cody is the first to breach the subject.

I pour another stiff glass of whiskey, knowing it's going to be my last one for the night, and then glance up to both him and Brady. "I sure fucking hope so, boys."

"Heard you two have a daughter." He pours

himself another drink and then waves for the waitress to bring us over another bottle.

For the briefest of seconds, I bristle up on the inside at the question. It's my natural reaction. Shouldn't be, but it is. Of course, people are going to be curious and want to know. I take a long drink before answering him.

"We do. Her name is Whit, and she's freaking incredible. You'll have to come out and meet her." I slide my drink on the table at the same moment Jules strides up to me. She doesn't even think about taking the empty seat as Tessi slides in on the booth side. Jules curls up in my lap, reaching for her drink.

"You all are going to call me a sappy fuck." Cody twists his ball cap backward on his head. Jules reaches up and does the same to mine. "But I've thought about this moment for fucking years. The whole gang back together. Fucking right on."

"Cheers," the girls scream and raise their glasses. It's followed by a chorus of drunken giggles streaming from them.

Our glasses clink one more time tonight, cementing us together once again. Cody nailed it. We are all back together.

"Just Like Jesse James" by Cher begins strumming in the bar. Jules jumps up like her ass is on fire and goes for my hands.

"Come on. Come on, baby. We used to dance to this one all the time." She does her best to tug on my hand.

I've had enough alcohol to stand up and indulge my girl. Hell, I'd do it sober. She guides me out to the small make-shift dance floor. Once we are squared up in the middle and the only couple out there, Jules whips around, swaying her hips back and forth and holding one of my hands.

She uses her other hand to taunt me with the words of the songs. Never thought about them much back in the day, but Jesus, at this moment, they're everything. Jules snakes her way up to me, shaking everything the good Lord blessed her with.

She drops my hand, swaying back and forth for a few more beats, dragging her hands up to her hair and closing her eyes as she gets lost in the song. Seeing this strong woman so carefree does something to me. I want to look at her like this every single damn day.

She finally wraps her arms around my neck, bringing her body up to mine. I let her lead. My hips find the same rhythm as hers. I glide my hands down her sides until they settle right above the globes of her ass. Jules smiles up at me with her eyes, mouthing every word of the song to me, enticing a battle of breaking hearts and who will be the strongest in the end. She's all in. I have no doubt anymore.

I drop my forehead to hers, singing right back, matching her word for word. We promise each other the world in a complicated dance. During a break in the song, I reach down and catch her plump bottom lip between my teeth. Jules pulls back and captures my lips with hers. We get lost in each other. Tongues tango, teeth collide as we soak up every ounce of each other. Her taste dances on my tongue, leaving me craving more of her. There will never be enough. Jules reaches up, plucks my hat from my head, and places it on hers without breaking the kiss. My hands move on instinct from her back to cup her cheeks. It's an act of keeping her in this place forever. Our hips never quit moving to the music as we devour each other.

The song ends, and "Heaven" by Kane Brown serenades us. I smile against her lips, breaking our kiss.

"What's so funny?" She pulls back just enough to ask the question.

I shake my head, kissing the tip of her nose. "Nothing. I couldn't figure out how to describe this moment in my head."

"And?" She tilts her head.

"It's heaven. I know what perfection and absolute joy feel like."

Jules smiles and drops the side of her cheek to my chest. My hands roam back down, and we soak up each word of the song in unison. It's the two of us who exist in the crowded bar. The way it should be. The way it always will be.

The bar erupts in cheers as the song ends. Jules buries her face in my chest. I kiss the top of her head, keeping her safe and protected against me. It's always been my job, and I'll never lose that responsibility again.

"I Will Wait" by Mumford & Sons begins jamming. Tessi drags Brady out on the dance floor, and Cody pulls a random woman out as well.

"Sorry, Jules. I love this song," Tessi hollers over the speakers.

Jules waves her off then glances up at me. A

smile covers her face then laughter ensues.

"What?" I lean down and whisper in her ear.

"This song," she hollers back up to me.

I quirk an eyebrow in question. Jules perches up on her tiptoes. More bodies have surrounded us, so I take it upon myself to lift her up by the hips until her legs wrap tight around my center.

She presses her cheek against mine. Her lips glide up and down the shell of my ear. "The song. I've waited, Jessie. I haven't been with another man. I tried dating but never got over you."

Chapter 17

Jules

My head fogs with delightful confusion and relaxation. I'm not too far gone. I know what I'm doing and damn well know I'd do it sober. Three more drinks and I'd be flat-ass drunk.

Or that's what I thought until I wrapped myself up in Jessie. His scent, warmth, and touch destroyed me. I was immediately intoxicated. I drowned in a state I never wanted to escape from. I now understand the lure of being an addict. I fully accept it and have no shame.

The sweat beads pour off my forehead. The array of music was intense from old pop, romantic songs, then right into downhome country swinging music. I danced to it all with Jessie at my side. My legs screamed in agony, and sweat coated every inch of my body and clothing. All in all, it was a pathetic, disgusting scene and exhilarating at the same time. The dancing and contact were better than jumping out of a plane or facing an alligator. It was so much more.

"Here you all go." Cody slings a tray of waters, more Jack Daniels, and a pitcher of Pussy Pleasers on the center of the table.

The crowd has died down. Only the die-hards are left behind. I'm able to make a few out. Instead of aging five to eight years, it seems they've added twenty on. They stare, point, and whisper, but I couldn't give a shit tonight. It seems a tinge of magic has sprinkled down on us. I'm floating on cloud nine, and it's not the booze. It's Jessie.

"One final toast." Jessie situates everyone's drinks.

He pours mine first and makes sure it's right in front of me. I sit back further into him with my arm wrapped around his neck. Everyone else grabs theirs and waits on Jessie. He didn't have to tell me earlier that my toast got to him. I could see on his features. I swear to God, I can still read the man like an open book. Hell, I could write him as the main character with my eyes closed.

Jessie clears his throat then raises his glass with nothing but confidence. "To my friends. To my family. To my love and to my daughter. I made one horrible choice years ago where I could've lost everything, but by the grace of God, I was blessed with one last chance where I'll never have to regret the yesterdays because all the yesterdays are gone."

The jukebox cuts off. A deathly silence floats around the table. We all take in his words. Jessie just admitted aloud to others our past sins that have in the end turned out to be nothing but beauty.

"Cheers." I raise my glass, my voice filled with

nothing but confidence.

"Cheers," the rest of our friends echo.

Our glasses clink together, cementing all of our futures. I have no doubt where my home will always be. It's here with this man. Now, it's time to build up the courage to believe this sentiment every second of my day, never letting doubt or the past linger in again.

I finish off my final glass of Pussy Pleaser, ironic as it is since nothing has pleased anything downtown since Whit was conceived. Cody goes about cleaning up the bar while the rest of us nurse waters, knowing damn well we will all have wicked hangovers in the morning. Or at least I will. The saying "I'll never drink again" always fails. But it was one hell of a night.

"Home fries." Cody bounds back up to the table. He's like a damn night owl all energetic and ready to start the day. You'd think he was going on his third cup of coffee. "I've got two damn good kids here who are my dishwashers. They're pretty much the same as fucking Uber but in a Podunk town, no tips required. Tell them where you want to end up, and they'll take you. Their girlfriends will follow, and then they'll go boink until the sunrise. I've got their backs, so their parents truly do believe I've worked their asses off all night long when in reality they are getting a piece of ass themselves."

I groan and cover my eyes as if it was live action going off before me. It was made ten times worse when the young boys stepped in front of us holding out their hands for our keys. Brady tossed his, overall too anxious to get going to pound town while Jessie had to dig around in his pocket. I blocked out the fact both of the men were way too comfortable with this scenario.

I don't get the opportunity to dwell on this fact since we are rushed out of the bar, and Cody tosses a brunette over his shoulder, smacking her ass on the way upstairs to his loft.

I'm wrapped up next to Jessie as the youngster drives us home. Jessie runs his hand down the length of my spine then massages out the back of my neck. He does this on repeat, making it impossible to keep my eyes open. Whether it be the booze or being drunk on my first and only love, my eyes flutter shut. Complete darkness settles upon me. I don't have a worry in the world is my last thought.

"Baby." My shoulder shakes. "We are home."

A dim light fights like a little bitch to blind me, but I do my best to ignore it until the next shake comes.

"Jules, we are home." Jessie's gruff voice finally stirs me awake.

It takes me long moments to stretch out and wipe the sleep from my eyes. We are in Jessie's childhood home, and it's pitch black out.

"What time is it?" I ask, stretching while fighting the urge to curl right back up into Jessie's chest.

"It's four in the morning." He scoops me up and pops open the door to his truck. "I have one percent left on my phone. We need it to make it into the house."

I want to argue. But can't. I want to sleep and get an ice cold drink of water before I do so.

"Jessie?" I'm jostled around until I'm perched against his chest.

"Yeah." He adjusts me in his arms.

"Are you carrying me like a baby?" It's not what I wanted to ask but the only thing I can focus on.

"I guess so." The crunch of gravel sounds underneath his sneakers.

"This is romantic. You're about to carry me over the threshold like a groom does his wife." My voice echoes around the countryside.

"Shhh, baby, we're almost to the front."

"Going to chapel…gonna marry you." I hear the tune of the song perfectly in my head but know I'm slaughtering every single word. It doesn't matter; I continue on like the drunken badass I am. That last drink really hit me hard.

"I love you, Jules, but you need to quiet down a bit. We'll have the whole town awake at this point."

A creak cracks through the darkness. It's the screen door, and I remember I'm thirsty as fuck.

"Jessie," I try to whisper. It comes out so loud I scare myself.

"Jules," he hisses.

I reach up and grab his earlobe, tugging it down to my mouth and doing my best to whisper, "I'm thirsty."

"I love you. I really do," Jessie growls then slaps his hand over my mouth.

I kind of like it. In a weird and effed-up world, I could pretend he was an alpha alien about to make me his sex slave. My stomach lurches at the thought. How fucking drunk am I?

I catch a figure out of the corner of my eye. It's

Nana. I go to shout her name then remember the hand clutched over my mouth. She's passed out stone cold in her town clothes. I bet she got a round or two of Pussy Pleasers herself.

Oh no. Jesus, that causes my stomach to rebel again. I squirm and struggle in Jessie's arms.

"Hey, now. Hey." His pace picks up. "You're just fine."

Before I know it, I'm settled on the kitchen countertop with Jessie between my legs.

"Breathe. Relax, and I'll get you a bottle of water." He reaches over to the fridge, pulling out three of them.

I want to laugh because he said one. Jesus on a sandal, or is it Christ on a cracker; how many more drinks did I have? Jessie brings the bottle of water to my lips. I suck it down like it's liquid cocaine; hell, maybe it is at this point.

"Easy, you'll upset your stomach." Jessie screws the cap back on the bottle. "We're going up to my room."

"The one we boned in?" I ask excitedly.

He nods.

"Wait." I throw out my hand, nearly nailing him in the chin instead of his chest. "Did you nail, screw, or pile drive Shayna up there?"

He shakes his head. "She's never been at Mom and Dad's place. Wasn't her thing."

"Okay, let's go pile dirt up there."

Jessie shakes his head and bites down on his laughter.

I drop my forehead to the top of his shoulder. "I wasn't this drunk. What happened?"

He plucks the hair tie out of my hair then run his fingers through the long curls. "Babe, I'm thinking the last two Pussy Pleasers you and Tessi downed bit you in the ass."

"They taste like Kool-Aid," I mumble.

"Exactly. Those are the ones that kick your ass." His hands roam up and down my back.

A moment of clarity hits me. "Are you sure Whit is here?"

I remember Jessie telling me his mom texted him letting him know Whit and Jane were staying the night. Something about an epic spa party with both grandmas.

I grab the two water bottles and sling my arms around his neck in a sloppy-ass motion. Jessie clutches my ass, lifting me from the counter and making his way up the stairs. All of my goofy giddiness has disappeared as fast as it attacked me. My eyelids are heavy once again. All I want is a bed, Jessie's body wrapped around mine, and sleep.

Jessie stops at the opening of a door and peers in. Just enough moonlight blazes up the room. I clutch to Jessie tighter, seeing the view in front of us. His dad on one side of the bed, his mom in the middle, and my little monkey curled right up next to her. Fire engine red lipstick lines Whit's lips. I can only imagine what she got into tonight. I guarantee she had the best night of her life.

Jessie steps away and whispers in my ear. "Want me to move her to be with us?"

Any other time, it would've been a solid yes, but I shake my head no. Whit has found her family and is soaking up every second of it. The next thing I know, I'm gently laid back on Jessie's bed. I enjoy the view as he reaches behind his neck, stripping away his shirt. Next are his shorts until he's only clothed in a black pair of boxers.

I fumble with the button on my shorts. Jessie's hand covers mine. He glides them down smoothly and does the same with the rest of my clothes until I'm left in my pink panties. He walks over to a dresser, causing my heart to immediately sink.

"Sit up, baby. As much as I want those tits pressed up against me as we sleep, we better have a shirt on you because you know Whit will be bounding in." He eases me up, tugging the shirt over my head.

He's right. But damn, did the other scenario sound like perfection. I grab his hands, tugging him down to me. His body shelters mine. I spread my legs wide so he can settle in. His arms brace each side of my face with his hands clasped on the top of my head.

"Jules," he croaks out in a husky voice.

"Yeah." I bring a hand up to drag my finger along his jawline.

"I want you so bad." He pushes his center into mine.

"I want you, too."

"You're drunk, and I'm not quite sober," he murmurs into my lips. "And this is something we both need to remember every second of."

"And your parents, my nana, and our daughter," I add.

Our smiles press into each other, and then we both stifle our laughter.

"Just like back in high school," I whisper.

"It's better, Jules, so much fucking better. I'll never be able to explain it."

"Then show me." I press upon his shoulders.

Jessie picks up on my meaning, gliding right down my body. He growls when his nose glides along my panties. My hips buck up, wanting more. He takes his time taunting and teasing me until I'm dripping wet.

"Jessie," I moan, reaching down and gripping a fistful of his hair in my hand. "Please."

"Please what, baby?" he growls against my core. The vibrations race right up my spine, exploding behind my eyelids.

"Please, please, please," I chant, unable to get the rest out.

"Tell me," he growls again.

His gentle touch threatens to send me over the edge. It's been so many years since I've been touched.

"Make me feel you, Jessie, please."

With those simple words, my panties are pulled down my legs, the harsh material of the lace scraping my sensitive skin. It adds to the turmoil of lust, longing, and want brewing inside of me.

Jessie dips his head back down between my legs. His scruff borders on a full beard, adding to the sensation. I'm dripping wet, and Jessie wastes no time lapping it up, teasing my folds with his talented tongue. My hips beg for more, pushing up into his face as I continue to pull down on his hair.

His fingers join the seductive dance, and I'm gone. First one then two with his tongue swirling my bud and I lose all sense of control. Jessie reaches up with a free hand to cover my mouth when my cries begin to build up. He's relentless with his tongue, not giving me a second to process anything that's happening. All I know is my body is on a high that I never want to leave.

The build-up low in my core develops to a point where combustion is the only option. I dig my fingers into his hair and bite down on his hand as stars burst behind my eyelids. I'm throttled over the edge of a cliff, free-falling. It continues on and on until my body is exhausted and melts back into the bed.

I feel my panties glide back up my legs, and then Jessie body is on mine again. I'm in the process of catching my breath when his lips crash down on mine. He's aggressive, kissing the hell out of me and sharing my taste with me. I match his action move for move. His throbbing cock glides up my folds, taunting me and leaving me wanting more of Jessie. Screw being drunk and the fact our family surrounds us in this house.

"Jessie." I break the kiss. "Give me your cock. I need to taste you."

He drops his head down in the crook of my neck. His scruff tickles every inch of skin.

"No, baby, I want to end the night on a perfect note. And that was fucking perfection," he growls then maneuvers us until my head lies on the pillow with his body holding mine.

"Jessie," I whimper into his chest.

"Not tonight. Like I said, that was perfection. Go to sleep, baby girl. We have all of our tomorrows."

His hand runs up and down my spine.

I open my mouth to speak. I'm distracted as the hypnotic, soothing action lulls me to sleep. All I can think of is the word…tomorrows.

"Jules," Jessie whispers.

I'm dangerously bordering sleep and can't answer.

"Since you've come home," he continues in a hushed voice, "I've prayed every fucking night that you'll stay. I have no idea what is waiting for you back in California and have no right to ask. I'm a selfish bastard. But yet I pray every single night that you'll choose Boone and me. I have to have my girls. I have to."

Chapter 18

Jessie

"There you guys are!" A door slams open.

I pry open my eyes just in time to catch nipple and then feel Whit climbing up my backside. I tuck Jules' exposed tit in her shirt, hoping like hell it stays contained. I didn't even realize last night that I had given her one I cut up for practice. I roll on my back, beginning to stretch my arms over my head.

"Daddy!" Whit bounces on the end of the bed. She freezes when she sees her momma curled up next to me. Her face doesn't give me any clues on what she's thinking. She nibbles on her bottom lip just like her momma does.

"Whit, you okay?" I ask, bunching blankets up on the tent residing between my legs. That's the last topic of conversation I ever want to have with my daughter.

She points at her mom then back to me then to her. "Does this mean you guys are getting married and I get the pony?" She slaps her mouth with her tiny palms.

"Whit," Jules groans, opening her eyes.

I know damn well she can't be feeling like a champion this morning.

"We aren't getting married. Come here." She pats the bed between us.

Whit tiptoes up between the middle of us, twirls with her arms poised above her head, and gracefully plops down, nestling between us.

Jules winces, and there's no doubt she's battling a gnarly headache. Hell, I have one drumming a wicked beat in my skull right now.

"Whit, baby." I pat the top of her leg. "Your momma and I…"

I have nothing. No words come that could even begin to explain our situation. I can't even get it clear in my head, so there's no way in hell I could start to explain it to a little girl.

"Whit." Jules scoots her closer to her. "Your daddy and I knew each other a long time ago."

She nods. "Yep, you told me that, and Nana told me you guys were high school sweethearts, first loves, and did naughty things."

"Of course she did," Jules mutter. "Anyway, life took us apart, as we've explained to you."

Jules explained to me that she's had to reassure Whit over and over again about the new presence in her life. It's like a dream my girl wants to believe but is uncertain.

"Mom and Dad are going to try this. And do you know why?" Jules stokes a stray curl of Whit's hair.

"Because you want to buy me a pony?" She clutches her hands in front of her chest.

I can't help it. This is as serious of a conversation we will ever have, and my little girl has me throwing back my head and laughing my ass off.

"No pony and you've got to drop that. It's because of you, Whit. You've brought our love back to life. It's always been there. Life took us on different paths, but we found our way back. Because of you."

Even with the crushing news about the pony, Whit nods her head as if she's digesting each word and understanding all of it. Silence pierces between the two of us. I open my mouth to speak but again have nothing.

"This is going to be very new and different for all of us, okay, baby girl?" Jules tugs Whit to her side. "It's going to be very important that we communicate and talk when we are feeling weird or something is bothering us."

"Okay, Mommy."

I slink back in the bed, rubbing Whit's back. "Your mom is right, sweetie. You can talk to me or your mom, Nana, and even Grandma and Grandpa, okay?"

She nods again. "If I had a puppy, I could talk to it when I was sad."

Jules groans. Before she has a chance to respond, my mom's voice rings up and down the hallway.

"Whit, want to help make breakfast?"

We both dodge out of the way as she rockets off the bed. "Do you have bacon, Grandma?"

Whit's voice ricochets off the walls, and I even wince.

"Sure do." Mom opens the door, sticking her head in. I don't miss the glorious smile covering her face. She more than anyone pushed me to try harder to find Jules. She always knew Jules was my one and true love.

"I'm in." Whit grabs my mom's hand, and they disappear.

"I swear," Jules groans, throwing her arm over her eyes. "That girl tests me every single day, and I'm never ever going to Cody's bar again."

I shake my head, caging in the roar of laughter. "I'm guessing you said that last time too, and it didn't stop you."

"Shut your mouth when you're talking to me, Jessie." Jules rolls to her side, propping her head on my chest and then roaming her hand up and down my abdomen. "And I blame all of Whit's damn persistence on you. That girl gets something in her head, and she never lets go."

"I don't do that." I grab her ass, bringing her closer to me.

"Liar. Remember the time you begged your parents for two weeks to go camping with a bunch of friends over spring break? Or what about the time you advocated and worked your ass off to buy that damn truck of yours?"

I shrug. "We know what we want."

"You could say that again," she murmurs.

"You forgot one thing."

"What's that?" She pops her head up off my chest with pain coating all of her features.

"You. I'll never surrender out of this battle."

Pots and pans commence banging and rattling

down in the kitchen. Soon Johnny Cash, Mom's favorite singer, begins blaring.

"Shoot me now, please." Jules hides her face in my chest.

"C'mon, let's get you a hot shower and then I have a pretty damn good hangover cure."

"I'm not getting up," she whines.

I don't argue. Instead, I roll up and off the bed. Jules buries her face in the mattress. I head into the bathroom of the room that used to be mine back in the day, firing up the shower, then I begin the task of dragging Jules out of the bed. She bats away my hands, fighting my every move. I revert to the fireman's hold, tossing her cute little ass over my shoulder. When she groans, I realize how wrong the decision is and the likelihood of my back being coated in vomit.

I'm way more careful as I settle her on the counter. Jules continues to swat my hands away. I bite down on my bottom lip as I pull off my t-shirt from her slender torso then work down her panties. Using the pad of my finger, I wipe away the smear of mascara lingering under eyes.

"Join me." She grabs my hand.

It's not a question, and I don't have to think twice about it. I leave her sitting on the counter, striding to the door to close it and lock it. Then my boxers come down. Steam billows out the top of the shower, the sound of the water pelting the shower floor serenading us.

"First thing." I eat up the distance between us, staring straight at her soul.

I sink down to my knees, spreading her legs,

craving her sweet honey taste again. I could've devoured her all night long. When the first taste of her sweet juices danced along my tongue, I was a goner. Nearly busted a nut in my boxers. Hell, I wouldn't have even been ashamed, either.

"Jessie," she gasps when my tongue glides between her folds. Her fingers twist and turn through my hair, pulling me closer to her. "God."

My fingertips dig into the sides of her ass, pulling her into me. This time I play her like a fiddle with my tongue sucking, nipping, and swirling until she's falling apart on my lips. I don't stop until all of her juices are lapped up.

"The water is going to get cold," I say, rising to my feet.

I have her in my arms and opening the shower door before she can say a word. The water has already turned warm. I don't let go of Jules until her feet hit the bottom of the shower. I fill my palm with a handful of Irish Spring body wash.

Jules tilts her head back, letting the water rain down on her. Her nipples point my direction, and I can't help myself. Ducking my head, the water streaming down my back, I swirl my tongue around her nipple, then I sink my teeth into the peaked bud.

Jules' moans fuel me on to pay her other nipple the same amount of attention.

"God, I love that smell," she whimpers. "I've kept a bar of Irish Spring hidden in my bathroom back in California."

Jesus, our love is so painful and raw. The power and velocity of it are enough to knock me on my ass. I ground myself in all things Jules and my future, gliding my palms up and down her sides until suds build up. I roam every inch of her body, spending extra time between her legs.

"My turn." Jules pushes on my chest, standing under the water and waiting until all the suds disappear down the drain.

I fill my palm with another generous amount of Irish Spring. Jules clutches my wrist as she sinks down to her knees. I can only watch in amazement. I open my mouth to stop her, but she's quicker, wrapping her hand around the base of my throbbing cock. Her lips hover over the head. A hissing sound comes from me as she glides her palm up and down my shaft. Jules darts her tongue out, swirling the head of my cock, licking up all the droplets of pre-cum glistening on the tip.

Then I nearly black out, unable to stare down at her any longer. I toss my head back, clenching my eyes shut, focusing on the radical sensation of Jules' hand and tongue working in unison. Teeth, lips, fast jerks, tender jerks, and then she cups my balls. My spine stiffens. A tingling sensation races up and down the backs of my legs.

"Baby," I grit out. "Gonna…"

I'm unable to get the rest of my warning out before I'm jetting in her mouth. My head spins, and lightning strikes behind my eyelids. When I peer down at her, I'm still spilling into her mouth.

"Fuck, Jules, so damn good," I groan, releasing the remaining remnants of my cum.

She licks the underside of my dick before popping off of it. Shudders roll up and down my body as she rises to her feet. My hands wrap around her, pulling her to me.

"Baby," I mumble into her lips. "I've never in my life cum that fucking hard. Jesus, Jules, you're going to be the death of me."

She pats my chest then roams her hands up, running her fingers through my growing beard. "Good, just the way I want it."

My cock kicks hard between us. There's no doubt in my mind that I could bend her over and have her five more times, but I'd only be half satisfied.

"I love you, Jules." I squeeze her ass in my hands. "I've never stopped, not one single day."

"We're doing this, Jessie. We are really doing this."

I don't miss the fact she didn't return the words. I'm okay with that. It's written all over her face. A shred of fear still lingers between us, and it will be my job to snap that and make it disappear forever.

"Welcome home, baby." I smile against her lips.

She grins right back. "I'm staying here. I won't be going back to California."

It's an announcement and one I've been dying to hear escape from her lips. It's better than any I love you's she could say.

"Thank you," I whisper. "We better get downstairs before we have visitors again."

She nods. I reach over and turn off the shower. I dry her off then swat her ass, ushering her out in the bedroom as I dry myself off. Jules is dressed in her outfit from last night by the time I slip into my shorts.

"Never thought I'd be doing a walk of shame at

this age and in front of Nana and my daughter." Jules glances at me over her shoulder.

"We never have followed the rules, baby." I walk up to her, wrapping my arms around her waist. She relaxes back into my chest, resting her head on my shoulder. We soak in the moments of silence and us.

It's cut short when we hear our names being hollered out from downstairs. I grab Jules' hand and lead her down. She tries to tug it away on instinct when we enter Mom's kitchen. I keep it clutched firmly in mine. A tinge of anger flares up deep down over her reaction.

***

Jules

Jessie's jaw ticks. I don't miss the sideways glare he shoots at me. I sink in my soul, feeling guilt. It's going to take time to adjust to all of this. I've spent the last years guarding my heart and raising my baby girl. My heart and body are all in. With just one taste of Jessie, I'll never be able to get enough. The rest will take time to learn to live again.

I exhale, and my shoulders relax. With that movement, I sink closer to Jessie's side, squeezing his hand in a move of reassurance.

"Momma!" Whit waves a spatula, sending pancake batter over the cupboards. Carolyn's house hasn't changed a bit. The same ceramic roosters perch on every surface along with the worn Formica countertops. I've stepped back in time, causing my head to spin with confusion.

"We made pancakes," Whit announces, her eyes going wide. "And some even have chocolate chips in them."

That sweet voice, innocent love of life, and round angelic face grounds me, reminding me of everything worth fighting for. Her happiness is my everything. I lean in and perch up on my tiptoes, kissing Jessie on the cheek before walking to Whit.

"Looks amazing." I hug her tight, ignoring the gooey pancake batter covering her front. "Let's get washed up and make you a plate."

Whit jumps down from the dark oak dining room table chair and slides it over to the sink. I help her adjust the temperature of the water and squirt some hand soap in her open palms.

"Nana, tell Daddy about our costumes," Whit hollers.

I cringe from an electric pain shooting through my skull. A hand lands on my hip, and a bottle of water and pills are before me.

"Take this, baby."

I turn to see Jessie with a puzzled look on his face, no doubt from Whit's announcement. I snag the pills from his hand and down them. I know exactly what my strong-willed and determined daughter is talking about.

I shut off the water, hand Whit a paper towel, and help her from the chair. I turn to see Nana sitting at the table in the same clothes from the night before. We sure are quite the pair. She sports a mischievous look on her face. I go to her and kiss the top of her head before taking a seat.

Jessie clears his throat, urging her on.

"Well, we got you and Whit signed up for the local talent show. After you two left last night, Whit picked out a song, designed the dance, and we…" She pauses to point at Carolyn, incriminating her as well. "…helped Whit order costumes online."

Jessie slumps into a seat next to me. Whit wasted no time climbing up into his lap. Tim, Jessie's dad, chuckles with amusement from the end of the table then goes back to reading the newspaper.

"Daddy, it's going to be perfect." Whit slides her plate over to me. I go about stacking it with all of her favorites. "I just know we are going to win, and I'll have enough money to buy a puppy and even buy a bed and toys for it."

"I'll just buy you a damn puppy," Jessie grunts.

This earns him a jab in the ribs courtesy of me.

She turns in his lap, tears building up in her eyes. "You don't want to do it with me?"

The table falls silent. Jessie is put right on the spot. And here comes a showdown between the two of them. My money, all of my money, is on Whit.

"It's not that at all, honey." He taps her nose. "I think you'd be just fine doing it on your own."

Whit's lower lip quivers. I reach over, soothing her back. "Hey, let's just have some breakfast."

She whips her head to me, flaming anger in her eyes. "You told me we had to talk about stuff, Momma. Were you just lying?"

I'm blown back by the tone of her voice and reddening cheeks. I stumble for words, having no idea where this outburst stems from.

"Okay." I nod. "I'm sorry."

"Whit," Jessie says in a low tone. "Go ahead."

"Forget about it." She wipes her hand under eyes. "You're probably too busy anyway."

"Whoa. Whoa." He stands up with her in his arms. "You need to calm down. Take a breath and relax."

He walks her into the living room. The floor plan of the house is open. The distance grants them privacy, but every word can still be heard.

"I'm not too busy, baby girl. I'm just a sucky dancer, and you're amazing. I'll just ruin it. That's where I was coming from."

"I want to go back to California," she replies.

My heart shatters like fragile glass in my beating chest. I jerk in my seat only to have Nana place a hand over mine.

"Let him handle this," she whispers.

"Why?" he asks, keeping his voice calm as the rising and falling ocean.

There are moments of silence before she answers. I can hear the sobs between each word she speaks. "Because at least there I knew I didn't have a daddy even though I wanted one for the daddy-daughter dances. Here I have one…"

"Whit." He stops her. "I'll dance my ass off for you. Hell, I'll dance down Main Street if you want me to. You hear me? I just didn't understand why you wanted me on the stage with you, and I'm warning you right now I suck, and that's the absolute only reason I was unsure about it."

Note to self: talk to Jessie about cussing while reassuring his daughter.

"Do you promise?" she asks.

"I promise."

"Pinky promise?"

"Double and triple pinky promise."

Silence thick as butter ticks by, driving me out of my skin. It takes everything inside of me to keep glued to this seat. My knuckles grow white from flexing my fists. This pain sheering my insides outpowers anything I've endured up until this point. Who would've thought letting someone else into your baby's life would be so challenging?

"Whit, honey, next time you feel that anger boiling up inside of you, there's a better way to express it. I'm going to tell you what I tell my players. Step back, think it through, and choose your words carefully, okay? That means not erupting into an angry fit. I know it's hard, and I still struggle with it as an adult, but it's something you need to practice."

"Okay, Daddy. I'm sorry."

"I know you are."

"But I'm also excited you want to dance with me."

"I'm honored to dance with you, sweet bug. Now let's go get our breakfast."

"Okay."

They walk back into the kitchen hand in hand. Whit wipes away a few stray tears.

"How about we take our plates and eat breakfast out on the porch? Just the two of us."

"I'd like that." Whit beams.

She carefully grabs her plate with her tongue angled out to the side in concentration. Jessie tosses a little of everything on his, tucks their silverware in his pocket, and grabs a large glass of orange juice.

Whit stares at him for a few beats before announcing, "I'll just share your orange juice, Daddy."

"Sounds good." Jessie offers me a sympathetic and hopeful smile. I know he's looking for reassurance. I give him a wink because in all honesty, I couldn't have done better myself with the way he handled the situation. I let out an exhale when the screen door slams shut. Their chatter is muted off in the distance. A few giggles can be heard.

"Am I screwing her up?" I rest my elbows on the table and bury my face in my hands, exposing my raw and honest fear. For the first time in forever, I don't care if everyone sitting at this table sees me as vulnerable and on the edge of cracking. I don't have any energy to muster up a brave face.

"No, my sweet girl." Carolyn sits next to me, wrapping me in a one-armed hug. "You're not at all. I'm afraid that's the game of parenting, always wondering if you're doing right."

"She's right," Nana adds. "It took a whole hell of a lot for you to stay in that seat and share the responsibility of raising Whit."

Tim clears his throat, and that's when I look up. His reading glasses perch low on the bridge of his nose. "It's like taming a wild colt. You never know what you'll get. One day a shadow won't spook them, and the next they're bucking you off their back. You go with it and learn the movements to stay on. And Jules, you're doing a damn good job of keeping in the saddle. Don't know any other woman that would give my boy a second chance."

"Momma," Whit hollers, running into the kitchen. "Come eat with us! Please."

And just like that, my feet are securely back in the stirrups.

Chapter 19

Jules

I've been damn successful hiding out at the farm until now. It's been a little over a month. My small family has a routine down pat. Jessie takes Whit to dance lessons three times a week; she loves going to football practice even though they've grown more intense with the season nearing; I stay home and write, help Nana around the house, and kick her out, forcing her to social functions.

She's done well getting back into the swing of things. She's had her fair share of breakdowns where I've discovered her crying into Papa's suit jackets or even sleeping with them. I don't say a word, only stand by her side, offering silent comfort.

I have no doubt the constant chatter and electric buzz Whit doles out has eased the grief for her, making it manageable. We've all become a well-oiled machine. I forced Jessie to make a list of needs for his house. The poor man is hardly ever there, but when he is, I guarantee there's not a damn stitch of food in the fridge since he spends his time working with Brady in the fields, coaching his team, and spending the rest of every single minute with Whit and me. There have been several nights where he's fallen asleep next to us in the bed and been gone in the morning. Other nights, he forces himself to leave before Whit goes to bed, and the pain that dances across his face crushes me.

I kill the engine of the car, take a deep breath, and clutch my purse to my chest. My insides whirl and flip in waves of anxiety that roll over every frayed nerve.

"It's a damn grocery store," I whisper to myself, swinging my legs out of the car and slamming the door with a bit too much force.

The soles of my teal Rocket Dog flip-flops slap the pavement, matching the drumming of my heart. This is flat-out ridiculous. I'm not a ten year old who's barely tall enough to ride the Zipper at the county fair; no, I'm an adult and avoiding the local grocery store at all cost.

I square my shoulders, stomp one foot on the mat to open the automatic door, and walk right in. I've swum through so much more murky waters than these. But this scenario has my knees knocking together. It was life back in the day to be examined under a magnifying lens, the ones you burn and sear people with. That's been aimed at my back for years. The only thing different is my papa isn't at my side encouraging me to keep my head held high and carry on. No matter how pissed off I was and geared up to aim hatred toward my victim, he'd tell me the same thing over and over.

"Firecracker, don't hate anyone. It's not worth your time."

I'd be stomping mad, and he'd deliver the message the same time and time again with no heightened emotion. It would only piss me off even more. Doors ensued slamming, and my 90's rock blared.

The crisp whirr of the air conditioning at the local market glides along my skin, sending goosebumps throughout. I dig around in the endless pool also called my purse until my fingertips glide along the shopping list.

"Shit." I whip the paper out and then bring my pointer finger to my lips, sucking on it to dull the ticking pain. Goddamn paper cuts. The most minuscule wound in the world yet the one that hurts the most. I nab a shopping cart with my free hand, sling my purse in the kiddy seat where Whit used to sit, and navigate to aisle one.

"Jesus, Nana," I murmur to myself, scanning all the damn spices she has listed on the paper. "Not gonna happen."

"Hey, honey. Are you okay?" Delores Dowd, town gossip extraordinaire, stops her cart right in front of mine. She's blatant about staring, analyzing every item in it.

"Hi." I take a tentative step forward and open my mouth to tell her to have a nice day, ignoring her other question completely. She damn well heard me talking to myself and doesn't need any more ammunition to gossip about around town.

"How's your little girl doing? She was so cute at

the diner. Man, she looks just like you and…" She taps her chin, continuing the parade of inquiring questions.

"She's fine, Delores." I grip the cart, my voice coming out forced and clipped.

"She's just a doll. I hear Carolyn is ecstatic learning she has a grandchild. It's just wonderful you've come back to town." She takes a step closer, barricading me between her cart and the aisle.

Screw me sideways. She's not going to relent. I nod, and she goes on.

"You know it's just wonderful you've let Jessie spend so much time with her. MaryAnn down at Gravy Dave's called it the first time you brought her in."

"Dolores." I hold my hand up, stopping her, then push her shopping cart out of my way. "I'm trying really hard right now not to be rude, but honestly you've left me with little to say that isn't rude. So, I suggest you walk away and leave me alone."

Her eyes go wide and her face pales, shocked as hell someone stood up to her. She's been used to running this town and the gossip chain. Well, it stops with me. It hurts more than I'd like to admit hearing it verbalized, even though I know damn well this has been going on since my tires hit Main Street the night I drove back in.

I go to the fresh fruit and veggies and dodge for that aisle, all the while sucking my finger and doing my best to avoid catching anyone's attention. This is fucking ridiculous. I pop my finger out of my mouth and grip the handle of the shopping cart. I square my shoulders and look straight ahead.

I push my cart past her and glance over my shoulder. "Oh, and Dolores—have a nice day."

The look on her face is one for the memory books. The old bat was left speechless in the middle of the local grocery store aisle.

The end of my cart rams into the stand of fresh cantaloupe, sending a few sailing into the air. Son of a bitch…the last thing I need is extra attention. I find myself silently snorting in laughter at the sight of the melons going up in the air. Ironic compared to my life right now. Everything has been turned upside down on its head. I do my best to gather them up. I kick a few under the produce stand because of my shorts biting into my abdomen. Nana's cooking has gone straight to my thighs. I brush my bangs out of the way, glancing over to the tomatoes. They look damn good.

I pluck the ripe tomatoes clumped together in a vine. They feel perfect. Once on a roll, I go for the onions, avocados, cucumbers, and heads of lettuce until every single fresh produce item is checked off Nana's list.

I skip over the meat section, chuckling to myself at the thought of Papa bitching me out. Even in California, he made sure that Whit and I had fresh beef, pork, chicken, and even fish. It was his business. The passion drove him to strive for more. The same passion catapulted him into politics, fighting for the rights of farmers and ranchers that produce food and so much more for all of us.

Just for the fun of it, I drag my fingertips along the cool, silky saran wrap of the meat. I find myself wondering if Papa would approve of the sirloin steaks, shoulder roasts, and tenderloins.

My spine stiffens, ripping me away from a nostalgic memory when a cackle and hushed murmurs trail right behind me. It's a damn ghost haunting my every move. I don't glance over my shoulder. I'd never forget that high-pitched bitch laugh even in my darkest of days. It's from the one who's tormented me since seventh grade. She'll always be my worst demon and rival who has the upper hand in every move. This time she won because she had Jessie.

"I would've put money on the fact he was going to propose that night."

"I know. Jessie told me he got cold feet when he saw how amazing the other proposal was."

The creak of the shopping cart's wheels echoes around the aisles as I continue to the soup aisle. The voices of my past repeat louder in my skull.

"I know. He's been insanely crazy over you for, what, eight or so months?"

"Susan, are you serious?" A resounding crash throttles the entire tiny market. "He's been mine since forever. Jessie's head got messed up with that bitch coming back to town."

Cream of mushroom, beef broth, flour, butter, yogurt, olives, and a loaf of bread.

It's the set of words on the list that repeats in my scattered, foggy brain. I hear everything, and it's the sole reason I didn't want to come out. I smile politely at some of Nana's church friends and other parents of my classmates as they pass by. My shoulders relax, and I thank God each time none of them stops to talk. It doesn't mean I don't hear the whispers of "that's her" or "I can't believe she's still here." All of the voices haunt me in my own living nightmare.

"I can't believe the way he looked at you at Cody's. I seriously thought Jessie was going to devour you. Remorse was written all over his face. This whole town has had Jessie and Jules married the day he was born, but we know who he really loves."

Check. I scan the list over and over again until I realize every single item is ticked off. I double and triple check that shit. I'm fighting to be brave as hell even though my fingers quake with each step. I stifle it all down, aiming my cart to the shortest checkout line.

We are armed with enough ingredients to make pot roast, tacos, barbecue burgers, and fresh salads each night with every meal. And that's all I need to know. I think about my daughter and smile as I lean on my cart, waiting for the next person to pay their bill for their groceries. Whit's toothy smile nibbling on a fresh ear of corn. Or her gathering veggies in Carolyn's garden. Those two are super hypersensitive over their produce, and that's why I'm sitting here with a cart full of veggies. Greedy little buggers. They've been promising us a home-cooked garden meal. The truth is those two find too much damn trouble, then my smart girl gets Nana involved, and there's no way Jessie and I could ever tell her no. These are the times we relax back in the rockers with a cocktail in our hands and smile. I lean on the cart, focusing on all the good. My future. My family. My life.

"She'll leave, Shayna. Jules trapped Jessie. We all knew she could, and here she's back years later, lacing the noose around his neck. Stay strong, sister."

I keep my gaze forward and can tell the two bimbos are clutching hands as if in a silent prayer to God, who would answer their desperation. Curiosity begins stinging my senses. I'm dying to know if they're talking overly loud because they know I'm here or it it's just their natural, annoying tendency.

"Number?"

I clear my throat. "Excuse me?"

"Number."

I sweep my bangs out of my eyes even though there's no hair to sweep back. My glasses are propped up there.

"Do you have a phone number?" The teen hitches a hand on her hip and gives me all her sass that her momma bestowed her with.

I lean onto the stand and then relax back again. I think about it once then twice, having no clue if Nana and Papa kept my childhood home number. I drum my fingernails on the counter and go for it.

She plucks in the numbers, a beep sounds, and then she begins scanning items. The voices don't die out. No, I'm not that lucky at all. In fact, more voices join in the Shayna-Jessie parade.

"He has a ring. I saw it a few days before she came back into town," Shayna announces. "I didn't even get the chance to tell him I'm expecting."

"I knew it," a random voice sings out.

"Oh my God, congratulations!" a chorus of voices ring out.

My spine goes numb. My bottom lip pierces with pain. I release my lip from my teeth, not even realizing I'd been biting down on it. My world falls out from underneath me, yet my stubborn legs refuse to give in.

"Your baby will be perfection. I'm so damn excited for you, Shayna."

"See, it'll just take time," another voice sounds. "Jessie's world has been rattled. He's always been a great guy and will come back."

Bile at the thought of Jessie being the hometown hero rises in the back of my throat. Some things never change.

"Yeah, so pathetic Jules had to drag a kid into this. I mean, why keep her away from Jessie all these years only to dangle her in front of him? I'm just crushed finding out I'm pregnant and Jessie is off doing the right thing." I recognize Shayna's voice.

The cashier gives me a total. I pass over my debit card, not even knowing if it was one hundred or one thousand dollars. Hell, I could've just won a million dollars and would have no clue. My blood simmers over into a boiling point.

"I'd put all my money on a bet that thing of Jules isn't even Jessie's. Well played by Jules. She knows how to pull at those heartstrings," Shayna announces.

"Oh, but have you seen her…"

I don't hear the rest. The ringing in my ears pitches out every single sound. My shoulder pile drives into the magazine rack as I round the corner of the checkout stand. I come face to face with

Shayna. She pales, only causing my blood pressure to skyrocket. The rest of the women pick up on her facial cue and whip around to face me.

I plant a hand on my hip. "Just thought I'd join the daily conversation here at Country Cousin's grocery store. Anyone want to fill me in on what I missed out on?"

Not one single word. None of the cowards are even brave enough to open their mouths to respond, so I take it upon myself to go on.

I take a step forward, leaving no room between Shayna and myself. "I have no problem with you calling me every name in the book and campaigning to the county that you and Jessie are perfect for each other. Not one single problem with it at all. Where I draw the line with permanent ink is when you bring my daughter into it. That's when we have a problem, Shayna."

She stumbles over some words that come out as mumbles then takes a step back. I give her a good thirty seconds to recover, but when she can't muster up one word, I continue.

"Say one more word about my daughter and that over-processed hair of yours will be ripped out. She's a five-year-old innocent girl in this situation. You thinking you're all badass standing here talking about her only makes you a backward-pissing chicken shit also known as a spineless bitch."

Shayna's chin trembles. Her posse remains absolutely still and quiet.

"Is there anything about this you don't understand?" I jerk my head to the side.

Shayna finds the courage to shake her head from

side to side. I lean in so only she can hear because I'm in bitch mode like that.

"And don't worry your little head. I'll be sucking Jessie off for the rest of his days." With that, I spin on my heels and stomp back to the cashier to grab my debit card and groceries. You could hear a pin drop in the store. My heart pumps into overdrive. My ten seconds of badass bitch strides right out of the store and into the parking lot.

Once I'm in the front seat of my car, my hands begin to tremble, tears threaten to attack, and my bravado is long fucking gone. Anger and another old familiar feeling boils up inside of me. She's pregnant with Jessie's baby. A neon light reading Game Over flashes behind my eyes. I thought graduation night was the worst night of my life. I was so very wrong. The second time around was sweet. Sweeter than sweet. And now it's just a bitter memory tantalizing my tongue.

The miles tick by as the tears slide down my face. How dare those bitches shit talk my little girl? The insanity racing through my mind encourages me to turn around and beat the fuck out of Shayna and her whole damn crowd.

The closer I get to the lane that leads to Jessie's parents' house and mine, the more my anger takes over. Every square inch of my skin prickles with pure rage. Jessie sure did an excellent job of bullshitting the hell out of me about how he wasn't serious with Shayna. It took me time to digest he did have girlfriends after I left. And he had every right to do so. It was my choice not to. It took a whole lot of maturity to get over that grain of sand.

It irritated and rubbed me raw until I chose to let it go. Only for what? To have it thrown back in my face in public.

Just a relationship to appease everyone and pass the time, my ass. He had a fucking ring. I can't even.

I slow down when I near Carolyn's house, peering down the short lane only to see Whit waving from the garden. What in the hell? She's supposed to be at football practice with Jessie. I pull the car in the lane and have my piece of perfection jumping up in my lap the moment I open the door.

"Mommy! We have radishes." She squeezes my cheeks with dirty garden hands.

"Awesome." I lean forward and kiss her, relaxing from having her on my lap. "Why aren't you with Daddy?"

"Grandma and Nana are taking me to dance. He said he'd text you to let you know. We are waiting for Nana to get back from town."

"Oh, okay." I do my best to act in mommy mode, concealing all of my emotions. Back in California, it was a routine I had perfected, but over these past few weeks, I've lost the talent it takes to pull it off.

"See, Momma?" She reaches over, digging around in the console, and holds my cell phone up to me. "He texted you."

I shake my head. "Silly mom. I guess I was too distracted."

"Momma!" she shouts even though she's sitting right on my lap. Her back hits the horn, blaring it for a few seconds before she sits forward, slaps a hand over mouth, and giggles.

"What, baby girl?"

"Daddy has an awesome fort here. Do you want to see it?" She throws her arms out to her side. "It's so, so, so big."

"Sure." I muster up a smile and set her on the ground. The last thing I want to see is some damn overpriced fort that Jessie built for Whit. I'll have to hold myself back from burning it down only because Jessie had his hands on it. Once again, I remind myself to go into mommy mode, swallowing down my emotions and feelings.

"Grandma, I'll be right back. Taking Momma to the fort." Whit skips in front of me along a dirt path behind the house.

"Oh, Whit, I'm not sure…" Her words die off in her mouth when she sees her granddaughter's excitement. "Go on."

I don't miss the fact the look on her face is resigned. She's tentative about this, and that makes me nervous as hell. Tingles race up my spine as if I'm about to walk into a hornet's nest.

"Just over this hill, Momma." Whit waves me on.

I turn back to see Carolyn in her garden and can barely make out the roof of Nana's place. The view from the top of this hill takes my breath away. I remember playing back here when I was little but never realized the magic of it. It's perfection, giving views from every angle of the best pieces of this area.

"Look, Momma!" Whit tugs on my hand and points.

I follow her little finger and gasp. My hand slaps over my mouth and eyes go wide.

"It's the biggest fort ever. Daddy said I could play in it if Grandma or an adult is with me, and I just have to watch out for nails because if I step on one, I have to get a tennis shot."

My jaw remains slack, and I can't produce one single word. The gorgeous framework of a two-story ranch house with a wrap-around porch slaps me in the face. He had a ring for Shayna and was building a home until I came back to town. I held the one trump card that put everything on pause permanently. For a few ticks of seconds, my heart hurts for Shayna and everything I ruined for her.

A garden that easily beats out his mom's lies a few feet away from the house. It's surrounded by wildflowers spraying up everywhere. A white picket fence borders the entire property. Blood, sweat, and tears have been put into making this place magical even though the house is only a framework.

"Come see it." Whit tugs my hand again, leading me down the pathway.

Numbness washes over me. I'm unable to digest a damn thing. The anger and hurt that attacked me minutes earlier dissipates. My heart aches and soul longs for what could've been if I'd smacked Jessie and told him to think about it instead of running like a scared and hurt teenager. I ruined everything at that moment.

Whit leads me through each room, giving me the grand tour. I miss it all. It's fuzz that buzzes through my head. Radio static at its best blares in my ears.

"Whit." Jessie's voice echoes through the frame of the fresh wood. "Whit."

She lets go of my hand and races out to the front porch, waving like a little mad woman. I follow her, not knowing what else to do.

"Daddy, I'm here. I have an adult and don't need that tennis shot."

His throaty and deep chuckle echoes in my chest. "Come here. Race up to the top of the hill. Your ride awaits for dance, my little bit."

"Coming, Daddy." She pushes off the railing, bumps into me, peering up at me with pursed lips. "Love you, Momma. I'll be back for dinner."

She races off, her tutu flowing in the wind along with her dark curls bouncing off of her back. This could all be hers only if I would've fought for her. I didn't. I ran like a coward and gave her the best life I possibly could. Jessie built this for his future, and that was Shayna. He had to be in deeply love with her to dedicate all of this time to a project.

I collapse down on the front step, letting the emotions of the day finally flow free. My palms catch every single tear—bitter, salty reminders of what could've been and never will be. I lose track of time. Hell, five or fifty minutes could've drifted by when I hear the crunching of footsteps nearing me.

"Jules."

I glance up to see Jessie in a tight shirt, gym shorts, and his snapback on backward. He reaches up to his neck, massaging out tension. I stare at him, not saying a word.

"I should've told you, Jules."

Chapter 20

Jessie

"Mom." I hop out of my truck and slam the door. I raced home in hopes of seeing Whit before they left for dance. She was a persistent little shit about wanting her nana and grandma to take her to dance. It sounds ridiculous, but it was like dropping my little girl off on her first day of school.

"Over here, Jessie." She waves from the garden.

"Where's Whit? Is she ready for dance?" I glance down at my watch. "You guys have twenty minutes. Did you put snacks in her bag? She likes chocolate pudding."

"Jessie." Mom raises her hand and voice at me. "We are leaving as soon as Jane gets here. Whit took Jules up to your house. I'm sorry, but there was no way of stopping her."

"Fuck." I kick at a stray rock. "How long have they been up there?"

"Ten minutes or so."

"Son of a bitch," I hiss.

"Language, Jessie!" she scolds. "Go get Whit so we can leave for dance. I see the dust coming down the lane. It has to be Jane."

I take off without thinking, fearing the worst. This is way too big of a damn shock. I know beyond a doubt it will scare Jules off for good. It's stable and a foundation and something I'll never be able to explain away.

"Whit," I holler out. When there's no response, I call out her name again.

Then there she is calling out, "Daddy." My entire body relaxes seeing her sweet face in the distance and having her voice singing in my ears.

I call her over for dance. She kisses her momma and races up the hill.

"Daddy, I showed Momma." Her arms pump as fast as they can as she races up the hill. "I even told her the rules about adults and the tennis shot."

"Tetanus shot, honey, and good job." I bring her up to my chest. Her little heart pounds against mine. Her toothy grin brightens my day. No matter how shitty of a day it is, this little girl will always make everything better.

"We have to get you to dance." I kiss her forehead.

"Daddy, I don't want to use up all my energies. Can you?" She looks down at my mom in the garden.

"You do know that back in the day I was the fastest in town, right? Hold on!" I bolt down the hill. Not as fast as I used to be but still getting the job done. Whit's squeals of laughter fuel me on.

I don't comprehend the rattling coming from my

mom. I make sure Whit is dusted off, buckled in, and has her dance bag with her. I shower her with kisses and then wave as the van pulls out. I'm tempted to follow them into town in my truck, not because I don't trust my mom and Jane but because I don't want to miss a minute with Whit.

But there's Jules, who is sitting down at my biggest secret to date. It was the place I could pour my everything into and get lost in the future I wanted. I jog back up the hill and slow to a walk when I see her hunched over on the porch with her face buried in her hands.

"Fuck," I hiss out.

This is the nail in the coffin that will end us. The push that went a little too far, sending her right over the cliff back to California. My own fuck up that ruined it all. A fantasy that I never thought would turn into reality.

"Jules." I reach back, gripping my neck.

She doesn't look up. Her palms absorb her sobs.

"Talk to me." I take a step closer. This gets her attention. Her wild brown hair flies up; her body lurches towards me with her finger pointing right in my direction.

"You motherfucker," she screams. "Why? Why lie? Do you think I'm that shallow of a person to rip your daughter away from you? Or do you just like playing games, Jessie? I mean, you can't play on the prestigious turf anymore, so why not play with my fucking heart?"

I take a step back, holding up both hands. "Jules."

"Don't even. Don't! You bring our daughter

here? The fucking place you built for Shayna and your baby? How fucking cute. Were you just planning to play house with your children and keep me a secret over the hill?" She advances on me, jabbing her finger in my chest. "I mean, do tell, Jessie, how was that all going to play out?"

"Jules, I have no idea what you are talking about," I say slowly. "I'm lost here, baby."

Her eyes flare with raw anger. "Baby? How fucking dare you call me that when you have a ring for her, built a house for her, and have a fucking baby on the way with her?"

My head jerks back in shock. What in the fuck is she talking about? I'm lost and drowning in my own personal sinkhole. I open my mouth to speak when my cell phone rings.

I grab it out of my pocket to silence it only to see Cody's name on the screen. I send him straight to voice mail. Elvis could be calling right now, and I'd do the same thing. Nothing matters in this moment, but this woman standing before me. Not one single damn thing.

"Let me guess, Shayna?" Jules stabs my chest with her finger again. I relish the touch because it's coming from her even though it's stemming from genuine anger.

"No," I growl.

My phone rings again, fueling the situation.

"Let me." She grabs the phone from my hand before I can deny her.

"Shayna, yeah, that's right, it's me, Jules. Talk to me, bitch. You've won so go on and celebrate. You got the ring, the house, and the most important thing, Jessie."

There's silence. A masculine voice streams from the phone speaker. My heart sinks for Jules. She's reached a sinking point, and I can only guess that Shayna had something to do with it. After all, she is the queen of fucking mind games. I should know this better than anyone. She pulled me in with her voodoo magic. I'm not innocent at all. I can think on my own and still drown in her.

"Cody?" Jules clutches the phone between her cheek and shoulder, wiping away the tears streaming down her face. "Are you sure? Say it again."

The silence once again drowns us.

"You have a video?" she asks, stepping back to the front steps to collapse on them.

More silence. I'm left kicking myself in the ass for not answering. I'd do anything to reach through that phone and rip Cody's head off even though he has nothing to do with this situation. He's the one comforting my woman. It's enough to send me right over the edge.

The gleam streaming off the metal head of the hammer entices me to grip my palm around the smooth wood and beat the shit out of something. I'm in the mood to tear anything or something to shreds in a split second. Every single muscle in my body screams and cheers me on to release this building tension.

"Okay, yeah. I don't even care anymore." Jules drops her head once again. "Whatever, if you want."

She ends the call and lets my phone crash to the

ground. My patience has done worn thin. I don't move slow but with precision like a man on a damn mission to save his fucking future.

"Jules," I bark.

Her head snaps up.

"What in the fuck is going on?" I demand.

She stands, doing her best to dip to the side.

"I don't fucking think so." I match her movement, keeping my hands tucked in my gym shorts. "What in the hell is going on?"

"Nothing."

"Bullshit." The veins in my neck pulse to life. "We can play this little sidestep all night long. I'm not moving until you talk."

"Jessie, let me go." She ducks her head, taking another step, doing her best to get past me.

"Let you go?" I roar, regretting the strength of my voice for a few seconds when she shudders. "How in the hell do you expect me to let you go when I've been holding onto your memory for years?"

This gets her attention. Those anger-fueled eyes glare daggers my way. Her cheeks are hot and flushed with anger. This time she doesn't sidestep me, waltzing right up into my personal space. That scent of hers attacks me, dulling the rage that had built up inside of me the last few seconds.

She flies up off the stairs, aiming that damn finger at me once again, ready to attack. Before she has the chance to open her mouth, I wrap my arms around her and tug her to my chest. Her fists do their best to pound against me. She fights for a few seconds before she gives in.

"I have no fucking clue what you're talking about, Jules. Listen to me. You can hate me, but all I ask is that you listen to me." I rest my chin on the top of her head. "I thought you'd flip when you saw this because it would scare you away, but I'm guessing that's not the case. I have no idea what happened today. But I'll tell you my side of the story. This house is yours. I poured the foundation the first year I returned to Boone. Little by little, I kept working on it. The manual labor of building, farming, and coaching became too much, so I focused on the landscaping then I'd go back to framing it. It's the house we picked out of a magazine our junior year. Remember the one we'd build after we both graduated college? It's that same floor plan. I never gave up hope. I may not have made the best decisions along the path of life, but the one thing I never gave up believing on was you and us."

Her sobs rattle between us. When they subside, she begins to speak, and it ruins me. "Shayna is pregnant. She announced it in the middle of the grocery store today along with bashing our daughter."

My fingers dig into her hips. The anger releasing through them overwhelms my senses. "Impossible."

"You never fucked her?" she asks, keeping her face tucked to my chest. The crass words coming from her lips take me back.

"I did." There's no way in hell I'd lie to her. "But not once without a condom."

I feel like a damn fifteen year old explaining my sex life to my parents. It sucks all the same. A shame like no other washes over me, one I deserve but sure in the hell don't want to experience.

"Cody has a video," she stutters out.

"Babe, I'm not putting the puzzle pieces together. Far from it. What in the fuck is going on?"

My cellphone dings on the ground. I don't want to let go of her but am forced to with my thirst to put this puzzle together. I grab the phone and steady myself to press play.

"She's not pregnant. It was a lie. Cody's lay from last night shared it with him. He swore he didn't know until then and has been trying to get hold of you but was slammed at the bar. Shayna lied. She's vicious. I guess some things never change."

I press play, turning up the volume on the video. It's the women's bathroom in Cody's bar, Shayna front and center peering at herself in the mirror. The camera moves, making the scene come in and out of focus, but the volume of voices are clear as day.

"That was so close. He damn near saw me drinking a Jack and Coke. I grabbed that bottle so damn fast," Shayna announces.

"Close call," a random voice adds.

"I grabbed that bottle of water like I was on fire!" Her evil laughter drifts throughout. "I have a doctor lined up that will tell Jessie I had a miscarriage. It seems he has a really bad marriage, and all it took was three times on my knees to convince him to help me out. He'll fake ultrasounds, heartbeats, and all the appointments up until five months. You damn well know Jessie will never turn his back on that."

My phone crashes on cement pavers before the video ends. I'm forced to take steps back from Jules. The rage streaming through me is out of control. Shayna never once wanted to come to my parents' home for dinner, we never once had unprotected sex, and I never fucking once told her I loved her. I was pacified and enjoying it, and now I'm fucked because of those actions.

"I get it," Jules' voice bursts through. "You built this for her, bought her a ring, and was ready to commit to Shayna until you learned you had a daughter."

"A ring?" I jerk my gaze up to hers. "Hers?"

This time Jules is stepping back. Smart move on her part because the last shred of control I've retained disappears. Her lower lip trembles, only pissing me off further. I'm not sure what else I have to fucking do to get through to this woman. She lets a few small-town whispers of gossip get to her, and she's ready to chuck us under the bus.

"The only fucking ring I know about it is the same one I bought our senior year. It was meant to be on your finger. Then I went and fucked everything up. I've carried it with me ever since. Shayna saw it in my dresser drawer and wasn't happy at all. That's the only ring she ever glimpsed while with me. There was never even a sliver of a promise of one from me to her. I screwed it all up years ago, and now it's evident there's nothing I can do to make it better or muster up a healthy relationship between us."

"Jessie, it freaked me out," she stammers.

I bend over and pick up a two by four, slinging it

right through the one and only window I'd installed. The glass shatters into pieces on impact, like my soul and heart does. Ironic as fuck. The blood, sweat, and tears I've put into this place are my demise and downfall. An evil laugh escapes me. There's nothing else to do.

I throw my hands up in the air after my tirade. "Guess that's all I do is freak you out, and that's all on me. I've caused this and now have to live with the damage. There's not one other thing I can do to convince you otherwise. It's like you're digging for a reason to run, Jules, and I can't stop you. So do what you will. Know I'll always be a part of Whit's life. I'd give anything to be a part of yours, but you can't accept it."

I turn my back on her and tromp over to the black mailbox with no name on it. It's never even received a piece of mail. It's ready to do its job yet has stood barren for years. I rip out the floor plans of the house along with the tattered page of the magazine from years ago.

"Here you go." I fling the paperwork her way. They scatter up into the winds and fall to the ground like a heap of broken ashes. "It was yours from day one. It's always been yours. I'll stay at the place I bought when I came back to town. You won't have to worry about me being around you. I'd like to still take Whit to dance and be a part of her life. Max will continue to come by and help on the farm."

I turn my back on Jules, crushed and devastated. I've put everything into correcting my wrongs to discover it's impossible. The frustration level has imploded into the point of walking away before more words are aimed, ammo tagging the heart as a bullseye.

"Jessie," she cries out.

I stop but don't turn around, waiting for what else she has to say.

"It all got to me. You never showed me this. Kept it a secret. I can't do this."

Her words obliterate that bullseye. I refuse to show weakness. "I hear you loud and clear, Jules. I'll pick up Whit for dance and practice for the talent show."

Chapter 21

Jules

"Momma, you need to SVRP for my birthday party." Whit slaps a glittered invitation in front of me.

I snap the lid of my MacBook shut and stare at the damn invite. I haven't spoken to Jessie since the great disaster I shouldn't mention. The healing wounds were torn open into seeping, raw scars that will never fade. One damn visit into Boone and my world imploded. How in the hell am I supposed to stay here? I have to for Nana and Whit's sake. But my heart and soul can't take it. Overreaction at its best.

I drag my fingertips over the sparkly ballerina, bringing the invitation to myself. Even though Whit's birthday is in January, Jessie has planned an epic party for her. I get it. He's making up for years that he's missed out on. He deserves this time, but it doesn't make it any easier to swallow.

"I will, sweet baby." I smile over at her.

Whit leans against me, flipping open the invitation. "You have to text this number, and there are gonna be seven ponies there and all my friends from dance."

I muster up a smile. "This is so amazing, baby girl. I can't wait."

I pluck up my cell phone and pretend to RSVP my spot to Jessie. It's all a façade. He damn well knows I'll be there even though my stubborn heart protests everything about it.

"Good job, Mommy. Daddy will be here to pick me up for dance."

Her words are cut off when footsteps sound on the porch. Whit claps her hands together.

"Max!" She runs over to the counter, snagging his plate of warmed-up food.

Whit has taken to Max since the day he paid for overpriced lemonade. She's been attached to his hip when he comes over to work. He asked her one night what she was having for dinner, and of course Whit divulged all the information. When she asked Max what he was having and he shrugged, Whit took it upon herself to make him a plate every night.

"Watch for your dad," I holler as the front screen door slams shut.

I haven't been able to write a single word since that night at Jessie's. A brick wall stares me right in the face. I can't even get out the word "the." It's pathetic and only adding to my anxiety. It's a billowing cloud of despair threatening to drown me, and all I want to do is run as fast as I can.

"I will," Whit hollers back.

I rise from my seat and go to the front porch to

watch my little ball of joy flit out to the field calling Max's name. The tall pasture grass tugs at her tutu but doesn't stop her. She loves it in Boone. Whit was always happy and content in California, but here she thrives. It's the rhythm of my life I'm still struggling with.

I lean on the pole of the porch, crossing my arms and watching her as she goes. It's the sweet innocence of her every move that inspires me and takes me back to a time when my heart beat for the same land. A smile graces my lips, and I relax.

The familiar roar of Jessie's truck nears me. I don't glance towards the ruckus, choosing to focus on Whit and her love for life. She hands Max the plate of food. He takes a seat on a log, ignoring the moving of the hand lines for a few minutes while he devours the plate of tacos and Spanish rice Whit brought him.

Max breaks my heart. Jessie wasn't exaggerating about his home life. The boy has nothing yet lives like he has it all. He works his ass off and appreciates everything given to him.

The moment Whit spots Jessie, she's sprinting to him with her little arms pumping as fast as they can. She leaps into her daddy's chest with her joyous squeals echoing all around the border of the ranch.

Inspiration strikes me at the core of my soul. My roots. This book I've been banging my head on the wall about has to go back to where my story started. My fingers need to pound out the happy, ugly, and every other memory in between. This tale deserves to bleed on the pages of the greatest story I've ever written.

Several more minutes pass before I turn to go back into the house. I flip open the lid of my MacBook. It was once my enemy and now my best friend.

Yesterday is Gone by J.J. Jones.

Once the first word fills the screen, it doesn't stop. My fingers grow numb, and my mind and soul are lost weaving the tale together. With each word and paragraph formed, hatred and insecurity vanish from my heart. I don't hear Jessie's truck roar back out of the driveway taking Whit to dance nor do I acknowledge Max when he tells Nan and I goodnight.

I stretch my back and crane my neck to the side. I have no idea how much time has passed since Jessie and Whit returned from dance. I can barely hear his deep baritone voice reading her a bedtime story. I creep up the stairs. I've never missed an opportunity to tuck her in no matter how hot the words flow.

"Daddy?"

Whit snuggles into Jessie's side. I drop my head on the door jamb, watching the two of them.

"Yeah?" He snaps shut the picture book, resting it on the nightstand.

"I thought you and Momma were gonna be boyfriend and girlfriend, and now you don't even talk."

He runs a hand through his dark hair. It's longer than usual, same as his beard, but I know the beard has a purpose with football season.

"It's…uh. I mean we are, but—"

"Daddy." Whit reaches up, stroking his beard.

"Just tell me the truth. I'm scared things are breaking apart again."

Jessie clears his throat. "Your mom and I had an argument. We are figuring things out. All you need to know is that I'll never give up on you or your mom because my love runs that deep."

She nods and balls herself up further into him. I take this moment to step into the room silently. I don't say a word as I take my spot opposite Jessie. We've done this several times since I've returned with Whit, our prized possession, poised between us.

Whit's tiny fingers find my hair, dragging lazy patterns through it. I kiss her cheek and relish in the sound of her calling me Momma. The poor girl is wiped like every other night in Boone. The girl is non-stop from gardening, helping cook, bouncing in and out of the house with Max, and everything in between.

"Love you, Whit," I whisper into her ear.

"Love you, Momma and Daddy." A ghost of a whisper rushes into the air. "I love all of this. Thank you."

And the idea of the book is cemented permanently in my heart. The words are powerful, and the strings of the story are everlasting. A legacy that deserves an endless tale.

I keep my gaze on Whit's chubby cheek, neglecting to peer at Jessie. I feel him inching on my skin even though he's not touching me. Once I'm satisfied Whit is out and I can't take the temptation of Jessie's scent any longer, I creep out of bed.

"I can go," he whispers.

The sound of his voice is a cannon straight to my healing heart. I shake my head then realize he can't make out the movement in the dark.

"I have work to do. You can stay as long as you'd like," I whisper right back.

Every inch of my skin craves to crawl back into bed and snuggle up into his scent. I have something I need to do before I'll ever be able to move on. My story deserves to be released from the clutches of my soul and live on forever. That's when I will be totally free.

***

"This is fucking weird," I say, turning to Nana.

"Watch your damn language. A lady never drops fuck like it's natural." She swats my forearm.

"Fucking really?" I banter back.

Nana does her best to stifle her smile, but it only lasts for a few seconds before she laughs. "It's weird. I won't lie, but completely amazing for Whit."

That's when I see her. She's dressed in a neon teal dress with all the tutu a little girl could ask for. A crooked crown adorns the top of her curls, and a dab of mud smears her cheek. Jessie is at her side passing out favor bags to all her friends from dance. The scene is too much. It doesn't make me nervous or give me the anxiety to run. Nope, it grounds me in place no matter how awkward it feels.

"Momma!" Whit waves her hand at me.

I wave right back and make my way over to her,

dodging all the gifts and children. I didn't even know there were this many children in Boone. I'm guessing Jessie paid off his football team to round them up.

"You look so pretty." I drop to my knees, spreading my arms wide open.

Her chin trembles as she barrels into my chest.

"Whoa, what's up? This is your party." I run soothing circles on her back.

"I wanted my momma here, and you and Daddy don't talk anymore. I was scared," she rushes out.

"Hey. You know I'll always be here." I can feel Jessie right next to us. "Your daddy and I are fine. We had to work through some things."

I pause and swallow down my pride. "Actually, Momma had to work on some things."

I fall back to my butt, pulling her into my lap, and Jessie follows. I reach over and grab his hand, offering a gentle smile.

"It's your birthday party that Daddy put together for you. Look at all of these friends from dance, and even Max is here. So dry up those tears and go enjoy your party, baby girl." I kiss the top of her head.

Jessie grip tightens around my hand in reassurance. Whit takes her time gathering herself together.

"Whit," Max hollers. "Time for the cupcake walk."

A few other football players flank him. Whit rushes toward Max with her near meltdown avoided.

"How many laps are they getting out of by doing

this?" I ask, keeping my gaze focused on Whit, who hops on a number and waits for the music to play.

"None." Jessie gruff voice melts me.

I look over at him, shading my eyes with my free hand. "Really?"

He nods. "Max and a few of the others saw me in the damn Barbie section at the store with a cart filled with everything from pink to purple and glitter covering my beard. I was way out of my element, and they stepped up to help. A few of them have younger sisters, so they took right over."

I drop his hand and twist on the grass, facing Jessie. "I'm sorry."

"Don't. Not today," he replies.

That hurt. I deserve it. "No, it needs to be said right now. I freaked out. It all became too much, and instead of believing in us, I let the past control me."

"I can't do…"

I scoot closer, cutting him off. "I've found help and have been pouring out the regret and hatred. It's helped me, Jessie. I'm sorry. I need to say that. You deserve an apology."

Jessie's body slumps in relief. The next thing I know he's tugging me into his lap, wrapping his arms low around my waist.

"Thank fuck," he whispers in my ear. "I love you so damn much, Jules, and was ready to give you as much time as you needed."

"Thank you." I turn my head to whisper into his lips.

"Your papa always told me you had the spirit of a wild horse. And it took time and distance to gain your trust or at least wait for you to cool down. I remembered our long talks in the barn throughout the years I waited for you to come back and grounded myself in them."

Hot tears sear the corners of my eyes. He may not be here in our lives, but Papa's lessons will always live among all of us.

"I'd like to go see the house tonight, Jessie." I drag a hand through his beard. "I remember the day we laid tangled up in the bed of your truck flipping through that magazine picking out our future house."

"Me too." He runs his nose along my neck.

"I can't believe you're building it."

"It kept me grounded, Jules. It was a way to pass the days waiting for you."

I relax into the safety of his embrace, growing drunk on his scent and watching our daughter live up every moment of her party. I wave at her when Max picks her up and settles her on top of a pristine white pony.

"You know you're never going to get her off that pony, right?" I break the silence between Jessie and me.

"She melts my heart, Jules."

"Mine too," I whisper.

We watch as her tutu flies in the wind, and she squeals with laughter as the pony trails endless circles. Max, ever the protector of the birthday princess, remains walking at her side. Whit waves to her nana, Carolyn, and Tim as she passes each time. They snap endless pictures of her. I remain cuddled in Jessie's lap, taking in the whole scene.

It's natural as can be, and at this moment I can absorb it with all my walls down.

"Final birthday present," Jessie announces, tossing his leg over the bench and heading into the house.

We've done it all. Cake, games, ponies, and more games. I had thought she had just opened her last birthday present, but I guess I was wrong. I was also confident the latest episode of Shopkins would be the hit of the party until Jessie brought out a large box wrapped in ballerina paper with a hot pink glitter bow poised on top of it.

"Here, baby girl." He sets the box gently on the tabletop then kisses the top of her head. "To all of your birthdays I missed."

A whimper escapes from the box, causing tears to spring alive in my eyes. Jessie has pulled out all the stops for his little girl. I want to be pissed off, but when Whit slaps her hands over her mouth then begins shredding the paper on the box, I melt.

Jessie avoids eye contact even though I stare him down. He runs his finger down his beard then trails it to the back of his neck, massaging out the worry. His t-shirt rises above his jeans, giving me a glimpse of his gorgeous skin. My throat grows dry. I'm distracted from my perusal when Whit squeals and a bark soon follows.

"Oh my God, Daddy!" Her high-pitch scream echoes around the front yard. The poor puppy in her hands backpedals, scared shitless. "A puppy!"

The poor ball of fur in her hands continues to squirm from shock and the noise level streaming from Whit. She doesn't pick up on the fright of the puppy, only brings it to her chest, squeezing the hell out of the blonde Corgi puppy.

"Daddy!" she screams again. "I'm in love."

I rise from the grass, dusting off my ass and sauntering over to the table. All of Whit's dance friends surround her, oohing and awing over the latest birthday gift. Whit hasn't let go of her new best friend, keeping the scared puppy clutched to her chest. God bless you, little dog.

"What are you going to name him?" one of her friends fires off.

Whit takes her time peering down into the eyes of the puppy. She then jerks her gaze up to Jessie.

"Daddy, is it a boy or a girl?"

Jessie clears his throat, not thrilled to be put on the spot. I'm sure he's backpedaling because of my reaction and what we've been through recently.

"A boy," he replies.

Whit looks back down at her new best friend. There are moments of silence before she speaks again. We all wait on pins and needles for the name. And trust me, Whit takes her time deciding, making it all that more epic.

"His name is Elliot!" Whit screams once again, shocking the hell out of the poor pup.

A chorus of cheers erupts, only frightening the puppy even more. Whit doesn't pick up on any of it. She's elated with her new buddy, clutching him tighter to her and kissing the top of his head.

"Grandma Carolyn and Grandpa Tim bought you everything you'll need." Jessie dips his hand down into the box, pulling out everything imaginable you'd need for a puppy.

And even though Elliot is a boy, they'd selected the most feminine items with sparkles and every elaborate design you could think of. Soon parents roll up, picking up their children and thanking Jessie. I stand back, soaking it all in even when the plastic tits of some moms get a little too close for comfort. Moments later, we are just left with Nana and Jessie's family along with his players cleaning up the remnants of the party.

"Whit, you need to let Elliot walk around a bit," Jessie says.

"No, Daddy, he's scared and needs me." She peers up at her towering dad.

Jessie sinks down to his knees, and the moment has arisen where Jessie has to disagree or at least tell his daughter no. "Baby, Elliot has been with his mother and siblings. This is a new environment, and he's a bit scared. You need to let him roam around. You can stay right by his side while he does."

"No, Daddy!" She clutches Elliot tighter to her. "He's scared."

Jessie gives in, plopping into the grass ass first. "He is scared. This is a new place for him. He needs to know he's safe."

Jessie pauses, scratching the beard on his chin. "It's like when you go with me but know your momma is close and everything is safe. Elliot needs to feel the same way."

"Daddy, I can't," she replies.

"Here." He reaches over, taking the puppy from her hands and placing him on the grass. "Just sit here and watch, baby."

Whit's tears roll on automatic. Her sobs escalate

until the sugar-riddled five year old nears break down mode.

"Come here, baby." Jessie scoops her up in his lap.

"You're going to take him away. I know it." Whit rattles on more nonsense until it sounds like a foreign language between her cries and gasps. It's sheer exhaustion from the excitement of the day.

"Elliot isn't going anywhere, baby girl. He's yours." Jessie rocks Whit back and forth in his lap. Elliot doesn't take any more than three steps away from them.

Soon enough, she quiets down, and Elliot braves climbing up into her lap. The smile that graces her lips will forever be cemented in my memory. When Whit and Elliot both pass out, Jessie carefully stands to his feet and takes them inside of the house.

I joined Max and the rest of the boys in the effort to pick up the disaster left behind. Once everything is tidied up, the boys give me a nod and head for their trucks, all of them except Max.

He clears his throat. "Thank you for having me, Jules."

"Anytime." I smile back. "You know Whit has deemed you her honorary brother."

A sweet blush covers his cheek. "You have no idea what it means to feel like part of a family. Thanks again, Jules."

The strong, young man leaves me speechless as he trots over to his truck of friends. The bravery and heart of Max have only encouraged me to find my own. After the old, rusty truck rolls out of the driveway, I waltz up the sidewalk and onto the porch.

The inside of Jessie's childhood home settles with silences. I push open the door to find Whit curled in a ball on the couch. She's still in her birthday outfit with Elliot snuggled up to her chest. Jessie rounds the corner, drying his hands off on a paper towel.

"Where's your mom?" I whisper.

"Washing up then going to catch up on *CSI*." He jerks his chin to the television.

I nod, catching on to what's going on. Nana rounds the corner with a glass of wine in her hand, giving me the same reassuring grin. She settles down in a recliner nestled next to the couch.

Jessie saunters up next to me, his large palms settling on my hips. "Want to take a walk?"

That desert feeling in my throat attacks once again. I'm only able to nod.

Chapter 22

Jules

The crisp breeze of the summer night whips across my face. It threatens to chill me to the core as we walk up over the hill. Jessie must sense it as he grips my hand tighter in his. The warmth of the action comforts me once again.

This time when I see the massive fort, my heart doesn't skitter in panic. My heart feels lighter. I see the picture in the magazine, the idol of our future dreams, and the fact Jessie made it a reality, or at least is in the process of doing so.

He leads me through every room, explaining all of the intricate details. It's as if I'm the girl years ago experiencing it all through the pages of a magazine while the love of my life holds me to his chest. I absorb each detail Jessie points out.

"What's this?" I point to a bundle of blankets and old chairs.

Jessie lets go of my hand, leaning back on a half wall, crossing his arms over his chest. "Mom brought a bunch of stuff up for Whit so when I'm working she can have a place to relax and play."

I scan the mound of blankets and the IKEA chair that folds out into a single bed. The love surrounding me overwhelms me. It's time. I've craved it for years. Now it's time to surrender.

I'm the first to move, stepping towards Jessie. He doesn't flinch or even move. He stands solid in his place like the first day I rolled into town. His intentions were always set and glaring in my face. It's time we seal this deal.

My fingertips glide across his strong, masculine forearms. He remains a statue before me. I take advantage of it, letting my fingertips drift through his beard. I trail them down his chest and further down until I'm roaming over his hardening dick. It fuels me on. I've waited years for this sensation. And now it's my time.

I perch up on my tiptoes, attacking his lips. Our tongues glide and dance against each other. It's all teeth and want merging. I grow drunk on the kiss. This sensation has nothing on the Pussy Pleaser.

My fingers fumble at the button of his jeans until I have them undone along with his zipper. My hand wraps around his hard, silky shaft. The next thing I know I'm on the bed of blankets with his body covering mine. My legs widen, and he settles between them.

"Are you sure?" Jessie manages to get out.

I don't answer with words and attack his lips with mine. I get lost in the mind-blowing kiss as we reunite fully after weeks of tangoing around the want and lust. Jessie's hand pulls away from my skirt to the side, and then the sound of my panties ripping echoes around the skeleton of the house.

"This won't last long," he hisses into my lips.

"I don't care." My fingernails dig into the flesh of his shoulder blades.

I feel him rub against my entrance then everything explodes inside of me. He moves slow and seductive. Each movement hypnotizes me into a better place I never want to leave. I dig deeper and mumble his name with each movement. The anticipation in my core builds and builds until it explodes, and that's when I scream out his name.

Jessie follows shortly. "Fuck, fuck, fuck Jules. God, it's only been you. I love you."

Then the warmth of our overpowering love coats my insides and runs down between us. I could panic and even freak out, but something inside of me tells me I'm home and it's okay.

Jessie relaxes down onto me with most of his weight balanced on his elbows. He drops his forehead to mine, and we remain that way for seconds, minutes, or hell, even hours.

"This is us," I murmur into his lips. "We've got this, Jessie."

I brush his hair away from his forehead. "I know I've said this before, but this time I'm all in, and I'll fight just as hard as you have."

His eyes flutter shut. "I've waited for years to hear those words since my fatal, dumbass mistake."

"You've got it," I reply.

"I've got everything," he growls.

He rolls off the top of me, taking me to his side. We both stare up at the skies through the rafters of our future home. The silence bathes and coats us into a soothing cocoon of forever. I cling to him with each beat of peace, and he does it right back.

The piercing ring of his phone obliterates our slice of happiness and forever. Jessie doesn't think before reaching over to grab it. I know from our time spent together it's a player on his team.

"This is Coach," he growls into the phone.

I'm pressed so close to his chest that I hear every word from the other end.

"Coach," a stuttering voice echoes out on the other end.

"Max?"

"She…she killed herself. She's gone." The sobs surround us. Max's despair shatters and wraps hurt around our hearts.

"Where are you?" Jessie jerks up, and I follow each of his movements as he rights all his clothes. I'm far enough away not to hear the response on the other end and only Jessie's. "We are on our way."

Jessie ends the call and tucks his phone in his pocket. I know the first half of the story, but not the rest. "Max went home to find his mom dead. He's at the hospital. I have to—"

I clutch his hand through his manic pacing. "We have to go. I'll drive."

Chapter 23

Jules

"Momma." Whit twirls her noodles around the twines of her fork. "Why doesn't Daddy come over for dinner anymore?"

Elliot races between my feet and underneath Whit's chair. Whit owns the dog's heart and soul, but when it comes to food, Elliot loves everyone.

I rinse the last pot from dinner, resting it on the towel next to the sink. "He's been super busy with football."

Whit's fork clatters to her plate, and I recognize my mistake within seconds.

"He's busy, Momma?"

I turn to Whit, going to her and dropping to my knees so we are eye to eye. I brush back the frizz around her ponytail.

"Yes, he's busy like when Momma has to be on her computer all the time. It's the same difference."

"Is it the busy where he's going to leave us again?" Her chin trembles.

I've failed as a mom. There's no way around it. Until this day, I'll never figure out how to tell a little girl how young and dumb Jessie and I were.

"He's working?" She tilts her head in question.

"Yes. This is like Daddy's deadline, and he has to put it all in."

"Like when you have to put all your words in?"

"Exactly!" I hug her tight to me. "I know beyond a shadow of a doubt that your daddy will be there for every single thing you do. He's just awesome like that." I brush a fingertip along her cheek. "And I love him so damn much. Daddy is a part of us."

Whit throws her arms around my neck; her spaghetti-scented breath tickles the nape of my neck. "So how about that pony?"

This makes me laugh hard, pulling her down onto the vinyl floor with me.

"No pony, baby girl."

And I damn well know that Jessie will have a pony in his daughter's life very soon. That's a secret I'll keep until it's exposed.

"But maybe in the tomorrows?" she asks, Whit now rubbing my back to reassure me.

"Maybe," I mumble into her sweetness, knowing that damn pony is coming very soon. Jessie has been researching and visiting ponies all over the local counties. He has to have the perfect one for Whit.

She nods enthusiastically. "He makes you happy, Momma."

"He does, but you know what?" I pause, ignoring all the emotions. "You make me even happier."

A horn blares, startling the both of us. Whit

beams at me. "It's Daddy!"

"Sure is."

She cups my cheeks. "It's our last rehearsal before the talent show. He has Max, Cody, Shawn, and Larry running lights and music like we are really on stage before tonight's performance."

"Are you excited?" I can't help but pick up on her enthusiasm.

"So much, Momma." Her gaze darts over to the pot of noodles still on the stovetop. "Can I take Max some paghetti? He's always hungry."

"Of course." I kiss her one more time before lifting her off my lap and standing up. Max has been living with Jessie since his mother passed. He's become a fixture in our household. I love him like he was my own son in the short time he's been in our lives. "Get your things ready for Daddy, and I'll get him a plate."

I catch movement out of the corner of my eye. It's Jessie leaning up against the wall watching us. Sneaky, sexy man. My insides pool and sink into lust, love, and forever. The man will always own me.

"Ready, Momma."

I finish sealing the aluminum foil around the edges of the thick paper plate before turning to my girl.

"Here's Max's food." I bend down, handing her the plate. "Go take it to him out in the pasture and tell him it's time to go."

Whit rushes out the door, making sure Max gets a plate of food before he heads over to the football field to run the light show for Whit and Jessie's last rehearsal. Their big performance is tonight right after the town parade that kicks off the county fair. It's the town's grand finale celebration, ending summer and jumping into fall.

Jessie and I have never been closer even though we haven't seen each other that much. He's been finishing up harvest while I've been pounding away the story of my life. The front door slams shut, and Jessie advances. I don't run, waiting eagerly until he has me in his arms.

"I swear to God time needs to slow down. I need you," he growls into my ear.

"I want you," I reply.

The next thing I know, my shorts are ripped down my legs, and he's entering me. The counter bites into the tender skin of my back as he thrusts inside of me. I bite and swallow down my growl, knowing time and distance aren't on our side. With each movement, I'm a goner. I fall, tumble, hell even dive head first over the edge, drowning in the ecstasy of forever.

"I'm about to go," he hisses into my ear as he pumps in and out of me.

"Me too. Please, Jessie, oh God, please," I chant out.

I melt between him and the counter. Jessie catches me as he releases inside of me. Time isn't our friend. We both know this. He steps back, cleaning up and righting his clothes. I'm left with his hot seed dripping down my thighs. I don't race or rush around to clean up. I can do that once he goes with Whit.

"See you at seven?" I wink.

"Yeah." He jerks and leans in for a quick kiss. "I hate this."

"It's okay, baby." I strum my fingers in his beard. "Everything will slow down soon, and remember, I'm not going anywhere."

"Thank you," he exhales.

"You do know I'll be recording the whole thing, right?" I change the subject.

"Wouldn't expect anything less." Jessie winks, turning his back on me.

I swat his ass as he walks away. His playful growl makes me laugh. His sexy voice echoes around the house as he calls for the kids from the porch.

It's time I put on my big girl panties and show this town I'm here to stay and that I belong to Jessie. I square my shoulders and keep self-doubt at bay.

"Elliot, let's get ready to go." I go to the laundry room, gathering his harness and leash. He may have been scared to death of Whit when he popped out of that box, but now he is her shadow.

I find his harness, strapping it on him, and gather the rest of my things. Nana is already down at the parade with the Red Hat Society. They named her Grand Marshall of the parade. It was a few nights spent with tears because we all know Papa would've been elated. Nana not so much. She was always in the background making things happen. So she called in her gals from the Red Hat, and it's going to be one hell of a parade.

Jessie's truck roars out of the lane. I barely catch the silhouettes of Jessie, Whit, and Max in the back window as the dust billows around them. I can't even begin to imagine what their dance routine is all about. Jessie and Whit have been tight-lipped about the damn song they're dancing to. I have no idea.

"Let's go, pup." I brush the fur of Elliot the same moment my phone rings.

It's Tessi, and there's no way I can deny her call. I know she's just as stressed out with her two little ones in the parade and in the talent show. Her children have claimed to be magicians, and I'm so excited to see all of it.

"Hey." I clutch the phone between my shoulder and neck as I adjust the harness on Elliot.

"Thank God you answered."

"I'm here." I smile through my words.

"What are you wearing?"

"Clothes," I respond, knowing exactly how psycho she is about this shit.

"Asshole. Like what are you wearing to the parade and rodeo? Are you getting all fancy or is it like a mom bun, yoga pants type of day?"

I peer down at my white Chucks, then up my tan legs to my cut-off shorts to my black tank top. "Um, just shorts and a tank."

"Do you have make-up on? Eyeliner? Is your hair done?"

"Tessi," I bark into the phone. "I do have make-up on, including eyeliner, brow definer, and lipstick. What in the hell is going on?"

"I need help," she huffs into the phone.

"I'll be there in five minutes."

Chapter 24

Jessie

"We've got this, Daddy." Whit clutches my hand, grinning up at me.

"Hell yeah, we do." I kneel down next to her.

"Hell yeah," she whispers.

Shit. I don't bother with the fatherly talk on not using that word. Whit is cool as a cucumber, and I'm a ball of nerves. I don't remember being this tied up with anxiety over any damn football game.

"I hope Momma doesn't eat too much of my candy from the parade." Whit nibbles on her bottom lip. "That was so fun, Daddy. I've never been to one."

I chuckle. She's eating up everything about the town celebration. I cannot wait to see her face tonight at the carnival.

"I'll buy you more if she does, baby girl." I hitch out a knee and pull her onto it. Whit relaxes back, resting her stiff, hair-sprayed hair on my shoulder, watching the other acts perform.

"I know you will, Daddy."

She remains silent through the next few acts, studying each and every one of them. They suck compared to what we have up our sleeves. My mom and Jane went all out on the costumes. It took everything inside of me not to bark a protest when they revealed them to me. It was the gleam of sheer happiness in Whit's eyes that held me back.

"We are almost up, Daddy." Whit slides off my knee, righting her signature tutu, then her tiny palms rest on the tops of my shoulders. "Remember to really shake your hips at that one part and don't forget your spin jump. You've been doing really good on those."

I smirk. "You got it, kid."

I reach for my cell phone to place it on the table before we go on stage.

"Hey, Whit, selfie time."

She lights up like a firework on the Fourth of July. My camera roll is filled with endless selfies of her cute face. It's her favorite thing to do. She's been begging for a phone for the sole purpose of taking selfies.

She leans back on my chest, props a hand on her hip with all the sass in the world, and smiles. The smile on my face is a mile wide. The gold chains around our necks shine in the picture. My sideways ball cap and gold tooth finish off my look. That's right—we are dressed up as hip-hop as it gets, right down to my MC Hammer pants.

"One more, then it's us!" Whit claps her hands together.

"Hey, I've got something for you." I reach back

down in my pocket and take a moment to clear my throat.

"Flowers for good luck? All dancers get flowers, Daddy."

Well, shit. Guess I'll know for next time.

I shake my head and open my palm to display a sterling silver bracelet with tiny ballerina dancers dangling off of it. "I love you so much, Whit, and wanted to give you something that you can wear to remind you of it everywhere you go."

I don't say anything else because I'm on the damn verge of tears.

"I love it." She wraps her arms around my neck. "And I love you."

***

Jules

"That was brutal." Tessi buries her face in her palms.

"It wasn't that bad." I shrug. "At least they had the courage to get up there."

"You don't have to sugar coat it. They put like ten minutes of their time into it. Pretty sure they just wanted up there on that stage."

"I'm thinking all the participants did that so far." I dig around Whit's candy bag until I find taffy.

All in all, this afternoon has been fabulous. Of course, there were stares and hushed whispers and even a few who had the audacity to ask about me and Jessie. It stemmed from curiosity and not a place of hate. It's only natural for that curiosity to turn into gossip in a small town, and I'm okay with that.

I check the program to see Whit and Jessie are up next. "I'm not going to lie, Tessi, I'm damn nervous. Whit and Jessie have been practicing a ton. She has high expectations, and we all know Jessie isn't the best dancer."

Tessi snorts. "Don't worry. Brady said that little Whit has been whipping Jessie into shape."

"Have you seen them practice?" I turn to her, slapping her shoulder.

"No." She raises both hands. "Brady has and told me about it."

Before I get a chance to grill her about every single detail, the lights on the stage black out. I feel a reassuring squeeze on my shoulder from behind me. I glance back to see Nana smiling brightly, sitting beside Tim and Carolyn, who both have their phones poised to record.

The light screeching of a microphone echoes through the auditorium. Butterflies swarm in my belly. I perch on the edge of my seat, chewing my fingernails, nervous as hell for the loves of my life.

A throat clears into the microphone, then Whit's sweet voice serenades the crowd. "I've learned in life that you just have to shake it off when you're feeling lonely, mad, or upset. I've had to do that a lot this summer, and that's why I picked this song to dance with my daddy. I hope you enjoy it."

The mic screeches again. Goosebumps race all over my skin, tingling with pride like I've never felt before. The lights flash back on, and the curtains dramatically open. I have no doubt that all of this was finely planned out by Jess and Whit. I can barely make out Max off to the right, running lights.

The first few fiery beats of "Shake It Off" by Taylor Swift begin pumping. There's an elated gasp from the crowd when Whit is thrown up onto the stage and lands on her feet. Jessie follows behind her, jumping up onto the stage, and then it's on. This is nothing like Whit's dance recitals back in California.

The front rows are up on their feet, intrigued by the performance. I hop up on mine and thank God Carolyn is recording this because it's hard to make out much through tears streaming down my face. A thick, roped gold chain is wrapped around Whit's neck, each one of her fingers are blinged out with rings, her hair styled perfectly in a side ponytail, a black leather jacket with a red shirt under it and finally her black tutu. The costume is wild and so perfect. Jessie matches in every aspect except the tutu.

During the chorus of the song, Jessie and Whit shake their hips and stomp their feet in perfect unison. Whit sways her hips back and forth, shaking her head at Jessie. He runs to the back of the stage, gives her a wink, and then does some kind of jump, twirl move, ending it by sliding on his knees right in front of Whit.

She ends the song with more stomps and dance moves. She hitches her boot up on Jessie's thigh, and they both cross their arms in unison as the final beat of the song plays.

The audience erupts in wild cheers. A line of Jessie's players walks up to the stage, and soon the two are showered in roses of every color. Whit leaps towards each one with a huge smile on her face. Jessie shakes his head. I know he's more than ready to be off that stage and out of that outfit, but he stays up there for his little girl.

When Whit collects the last rose, Jessie scoops her up in his arms. She waves to the crowd, who is still cheering and ahhing over their performance. Then just like it began, it ends with a dramatic sweep of the curtains.

"Jules, that was amazing." Tessi grabs my forearm.

I nod. "I have to go."

I sidestep down the row until I'm in the aisle. I remember this old auditorium like it was yesterday. I race down to the double doors that lead to the back of the stage. I shove and push through a few crowds of people until I'm backstage. I hear her giggle and Jessie's deep laugh. I follow it, growing more urgent as the seconds tick by.

I round a corner, and they come into view. Whit is still in her daddy's strong arms with the roses clutched to her chest and Max at their side.

"Momma!" she squeals when she catches sight of me. "Look what Max did. Daddy didn't know you're supposed to get dancers flowers, but Max did."

"Squirt, you told me every day about the flowers when I was changing water." Max tucks his hands in his pockets, blushing with embarrassment.

I take it up a step, wrapping my arms around Max and hugging the hell out of him. "Thank you, Max. You're a great kid and part of us."

"Awards," Whit squeals and squirms out of Jessie's arms. "Come on, Max. Let's go sit in the front row."

She grabs his hand and stares up at him.

"Oh, Momma."

"Yeah?" I grab her real quick for a hug.

"I don't want a pony anymore. I want Max to be my brother."

Max chokes, and I remain shocked for a bit. Jessie steps up behind me, pulling me back into his chest. "Done deal. Max is a part of this craziness and stuck with us."

I swallow down the emotions. "He sure is."

"Okay." Whit clutches back to his hand and leads him away, skipping. Poor Max remains shell-shocked.

He stops and looks back at us for a second. "I didn't tell her to say that. I may have hinted pretty hard for food in the beginning, but I had nothing to do with that."

Jessie's laughter vibrates off my back. I wave him off. "Max, you'll learn she's a force to be reckoned with. No worries."

"Awards." Whit tugs on his hand, and they disappear out the side door.

"So." Jessie dips his head into my neck. "What did you think?"

"I've never been prouder."

"My Church" by Maren Morris begins playing. Jessie and I find ourselves rocking back and forth in each other.

"Remember all our make-out sessions back here?"

"Fuck yes, I do," he growls into my neck.

"Five minutes until awards," a voice announces, then Maren begins singing again.

I turn in Jessie's arms, lacing my arms around his neck, his hands go to my waist, and we continue dancing to our own beat.

"Today has been the best day of my life." I run my hands through his hair peeking out of the ball cap.

He smiles wide. I throw my head back and laugh my ass off.

"You have to take that off." I reach for the gold cap on his front tooth.

"Hey, you're ruining my street cred here." He tugs me to his chest. "On a serious note, I was planning to do this tonight at the top of the Ferris wheel."

"Jessie." I pull back, staring up into those rich chocolate eyes.

"You always told me it was the only way you'd say yes. It had to be when we were on the Ferris wheel perched at the top looking over Boone. Thing is I can't wait a fucking second longer." Jessie reaches into his pocket then slips a ring on my finger. "I'm not even asking because you're mine and I'm never letting you go."

I glance down at the ring I picked out years ago to see it shine on my finger.

"Jessie." His name comes out in a broken whisper.

"Yeah?" He drops his lips to my forehead.

I continue to stare at our future perched on my finger. "I would've said yes if you had asked, but then you know that."

"Time for awards," a voice booms.

Jessie turns me around, so we are both facing the stage. I can make out Whit with a bag of cotton candy in the front row with Max and some of her dance friends. That girl is going to have the world's worst stomachache. We don't move, choosing to watch the awards from the side of the stage.

"First off, thank you for all the talent of Boone coming out and sharing it with us. It was a tough decision for our judges."

"Bullshit," Jessie hisses in my ear. "Those other acts sucked ass."

I pat his forearm and shake my head.

"First place will receive three hundred dollars." The announcer clears his throat. "And it seems this year R & R Ranch of Boone has generously donated a pony for first place."

A piercing squeal comes from the audience, and I have no doubt it was my daughter.

I freeze and whip around in Jessie's arms. "You didn't."

His smirk tells me he did. "Anything for my girls."

"Did you pay off the judges too? How did you know you'd win?"

"It runs in the blood, baby; we don't lose." He winks.

I roll my eyes and turn back to the awards.

"This year's Boone Talent Show winner goes to the very talented and entertaining Whit and Jessie…"

The announcer is cut off when the crowd goes

wild. Max leaps to his feet, hoisting Whit up on the stage, and I'm tugged out to the stage.

"Jessie, no, this is your win with her."

He stops cups my cheek. "Because of you. Now get your sexy ass out here."

Epilogue

Jules

"Whit, are you about ready to leave?" I holler down the hallway before entering my bedroom.

"Five seconds, Momma."

I set the pile of freshly folded clothes on the bed. A worn paperback gets my attention on Jessie's side of the bed. It's our book. He's read it over and over since the day I gave it to him and told him I'm an author. *Yesterday Is Gone* was written in a week and a half. My publisher fast-tracked it to get it out to the world. And to this day, it's been my best seller and is currently in production in Hollywood. My words will hit the big screens all across the nation in six months.

It's my second season being the wife of Boone's football head coach, a title that I'll always cherish and hold dear. Years stood between us truly becoming a family, so we didn't wait to plan a wedding, not even a small one. The courthouse, Whit, Nana, Jessie's parents, and our friends were the only things needed. Cody graciously hosted our reception at his bar, kicking out the public. Whit downed a dozen Shirley Temples that night, ending up sick and vomiting in a bathroom stall. Cody boasted it was the magic and charm of his bar. He went another step further, harassing Jessie about the fact in a matter of years she'd be puking because of alcohol and chasing men. It started a wrestling match that involved our wedding cake.

We moved into our home that Jessie built with his own hands a few months ago. It's taking time to settle in. The messes in every corner and still packed boxes don't make me flinch because I'm truly home.

"Momma, is this B crooked?" Whit bounds in the room, smiling. She's lost her two front teeth. I can never get enough of the cuteness. I pray they grow back in slowly because there's nothing cuter than a toothless little girl.

"No, looks good, honey." I grab our winter jackets out of the closet. "Go potty before we leave."

I swear Whit spends all her money at the Booster's club booth at every game. She owns every piece of Boone apparel even down to the face tattoos. She bleeds Boone school spirit. Her heart has truly found its home. Jessie hasn't given up on his little girl becoming an athlete. He hasn't verbalized the fact it would kill him if his daughter was a cheerleader. I know beyond a shadow of a doubt he will be her biggest fan even if it kills him.

Rustling then slight cries come from the crib in the corner of our bedroom.

"Perfect timing, little man." I peer down into the crib to see my precious, chubby dark-haired baby.

Jack grins and coos up at me when he sees me. I guess Jessie and I never learned life's basic lesson on getting knocked up. We were swept away with our intense love and longing for one another, never thinking about protection. And that was our best mistake because Jack was born in the middle of March. He's every bit his father's child. A damn near replica.

"Let's get you bundled up, little man, because when the sun goes down and those Friday night lights shine bright, it's going to get chilly."

"Momma, let's go. I'm going to be pissed if I miss the kick off." Whit hoists the diaper bag over her shoulder.

"Language," I warn.

"You know the rules." She winks at me. "Anyone can cuss when it's football season."

Damn, Jessie.

Bonus!

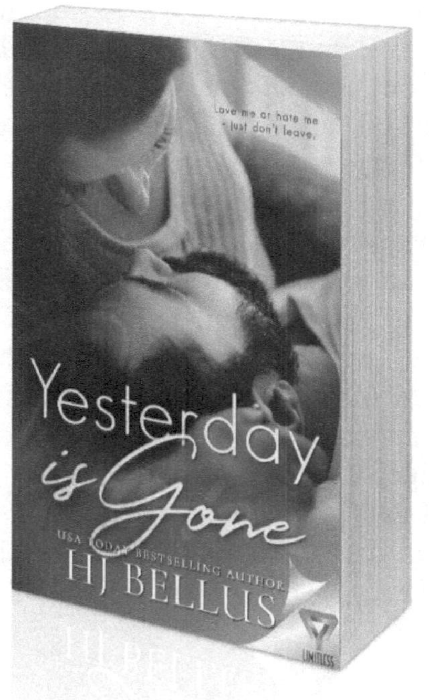

Get Instant Access to A "Secret" Bonus Chapter From Yesterday Is Gone by HJ Bellus Now!
Click HERE.

Playlist

This playlist embodies everything Jessie and Whit. I had it on repeat while writing and continue listening to it every single day. I hope you enjoy it.

These Boots-Eric Church
Smoke A Little Smoke-Eric Church
Jackson-Johnny Cash with June Carter Cash
Jessie's Girl-Rick Springfield
Good Directions-Billy Currington
Great Balls of Fire-Jerry Lewis
Pour Some Sugar On Me-Def Leppard
FourFiveSeconds-Rihanna and Kanye West and Paul McCartney
Just Like Jesse James-Cher
The Champion-Carrie Underwood
Broken Halos-Chris Stapleton
These Are My People-Rodney Atkins
Good Hearted Woman-Waylon Jennings & Willie Nelson
Soldier-Gavin DeGraw
You Look Like I Need A Drink-Justin Moore
I Will Wait-Mumford & Sons
Loving You Easy-Zac Brown Band
Say Something-Justin Timberlake feat. Chris Stapleton
If I Could Turn Back Time-Cher
Til My Last Day-Justin Moore
Flyin' Down a Back Road-Justin Moore
Tootsie Roll-69 Boyz
One Number Away-Luke Combs
Heaven-Kane Brown

Space Cowboy-Kacey Musgraves
You Make It Easy-Jason Aldean
Woman, Amen-Dierks Bentley
Cry Pretty-Carrie Underwood
I Was Jack (You Were Diane)-Jake Owen
A Little Dive Bar in Dahlonega-Ashley McBryde
I'd Be Jealous Too-Dustin Lynch
Rich-Maren Morris
He Stopped Loving Her Today-George Jones
Jack & Diane-John Mellencamp
My Church-Maren Morris
Diane-Cam
Broken Arrows-Avicii
Whatever It Takes-Imagine Dragons

Acknowledgments

As always, to my friends who are my readers. You make this happen every single damn time. Your love for the written word fuels me on. Thank you for taking a chance on a small town girl.

About the Author

HJ Bellus is a small-town girl who loves the art of storytelling. When not making readers laugh or cry, she's a part-time livestock wrangler that can be found in the middle of Idaho, shot gunning a beer while listening to some Miranda Lambert on her Beats and rocking out in her boots.

Join my newsletter:
http://bit.ly/2Lwofma

Facebook:
https://www.facebook.com/AuthorHjBellus

Twitter:
https://twitter.com/HJBellus

Goodreads:
https://www.goodreads.com/HJBellus

JOIN CRAVE